The Bookshop Hotel

a novella

 A. K. Klemm

grey gecko press

Text & Illustrations © 2015 by A. K. Klemm

Design © 2015 by Grey Gecko Press

Published by Grey Gecko Press, Katy, Texas.

www.greygeckopress.com

Printed in the United States of America

Library of Congress Cataloging-in-Publication Data
Klemm, A. K.
The bookshop hotel / A. K. Klemm
Library of Congress Control Number: 2015942794
ISBN   978-1-9388219-0-5
First Edition

This book is dedicated to Matty Salias,
for all those times we said we'd write a book
together and became friends instead.
Wish you were here to see it.

Part One

Sam's Deli Menu

Monday Special: Corned Beef Supreme

*Corned Beef, Cabbage, and Carrots dished lavishly on your choice
of either Sam's Homemade Toasted Rye Bread or Mrs. Finney's
Potato Bread with a drizzle of Au Jus Sauce.*

*Served with Deep-Fried Corn on the Cob, a dollop of Sour Cream,
and a tall glass of Iced Tea. (Diced Ham and Dill Casserole
may be added for $1.99 extra)*

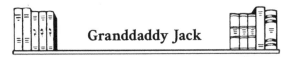

Granddaddy Jack

Abigail meticulously lined raspberry tarts and cream cheese Danish rolls in the glass case closest to the window facing Main Street and the Aspen Court cul-de-sac. Over the last few days, Abigail had been watching from the bakery as Jack's great granddaughter, AJ, worked on restoring the old hotel. AJ had been making her way around the grounds, making notes and bringing in construction workers while Abigail kneaded dough and mixed fillings.

Abigail wiped the flour off her leathered skin and went to the sink to wash up. A lock of silver hair fell in her eyes, and she scooped it back and started washing her hands all over again. The hot water felt good on her knotted knuckles. When she finished, she went back to the window to take a peek at AJ's progress.

Abigail had been a frequent visitor in Jack's home for decades, and she had watched AJ grow up. She remembered one day twenty years ago or so, when AJ was just learning to read and write, AJ had sat down with Jack at his writing desk in his bungalow, scribbling down notes for their dream project. Most little girls grow up doodling pictures of their dream house or of their wedding dress. Instead, AJ sat with Jack and planned out a bookshop.

Abigail remembered the little girl holding tight to Jack's pen while he helped her form letters over a sketch he'd made of the building in their shared notebook. Abigail loved that Jack paid no heed to the fact that the little girl was making a mess of the manuscript he'd been working on earlier that morning. For the first time in his life, Jack was running late on a deadline for a novel, and the publishers were hounding him. "It's just another book," he'd said. "This is my family."

That day was so vivid in Abigail's mind. It wasn't for any reason in particular that she recalled that day above all others. It was just a day that had stuck with her, a true testament to the man he had been: a broad smile and the glow of joy in the simplest of moments. There it was, Jack's smile. That's what this memory was about. Abigail had lingered in the doorway, watching Jack and AJ hard at work. "Maude says lunch is ready," Abigail had told him.

"But we're making a bookshop!" the five-year-old AJ had cried. "See, Ms. Abby?"

Jack had turned his face to the door, all wrinkles and smile lines and with a twinkle in his eye. That big, broad smile was why this memory was important. The whole town adored that man and his smile. Granddaddy Jack, everyone called him. He was known for many things, but above all, he was known for being AJ's great grandfather. To Abigail, he would always be her oldest and dearest friend.

Now, Abigail rubbed her aching knuckles. She got another glimpse of AJ, no longer the little girl of her memories, but a twenty-six-year-old woman hard at work on the building across the street. Watching her made Abigail feel her age. She was older than she'd ever imagined being, and her hands hurt. It wasn't good to be a baker with arthritis. It wasn't fair, but she supposed many things weren't fair.

It wasn't fair that Jack was gone. It wasn't fair that AJ was over there tromping around the property on Aspen Court alone. It wasn't fair, but maybe it was for the best, she thought as she watched the girl hard at work on the oldest piece of existing architecture in Lily Hollow.

AJ had inherited the old hotel on Aspen Court from Jack. Maude had been irked by the statement in the will that the old building would be passed to one Anna Jane Rhys, but when it came down to it, she didn't want the responsibility of restoration and resale. Jack had known that only AJ would see the old hotel his way, as something more than a property to fix up and sell to make a quick profit. His little AJ would make a project of it and open their dream.

The old hotel was four stories high with ten rooms per floor, except on the first, of course. Although the building didn't look extravagant or fancy from the outside, the first floor had an open lobby, a garden atrium, a restaurant-style dining room capable of seating a hundred, a kitchen to support said dining room, and a gift shop on the side.

There was a grand stairway to the first of the upstairs floors with a gorgeous red carpet on the stairs to protect the hardwood underneath. It was massive enough to see from every point of the ground floor except the garden atrium that led to the backyard, patio, and gardens. AJ remembered her grandfather telling her stories about the grand weddings that were held there by the "bluebloods" in the old days.

Chandeliers and art glamorous enough for the Victorian mansion-turned-hotel adorned all four floors. AJ would need an antiquarian art restoration company to take a look at them during the cleanup process of the old place before the grand opening of her bookstore. What she and Granddad Jack had planned before he died would be a thing of beauty.

The building had been boarded up and covered in dust for all of AJ's twenty-six years and most of her parents' lives as well. Granddad Jack had shown pictures and told stories of the hotel's glory days, how the governor of the state and his family had their reunion there every year and how all the rich and famous had thought of the place as proof of their status if an opening became available to them.

Rooms and weekends were bid on vigorously at charity events, and wealthy men paid for their sons to bring their new brides there for their honeymoons as though it were a fabulous resort. "It was busy but quiet," Granddad Jack had said. "That's why the rich liked it so much. It was quiet."

Now it was a ghost of what it had been, and it was AJ's personal mission to turn it into something new—a bookstore with optional employee housing. So convenient for the boss, she had thought, a lovely little employee perk, and finally, the rooms would be lived in again. This old hotel would reach back to all its past lives. It would service the community, make money, and be a home.

Each suite had a full bathroom with claw-foot porcelain tubs, and showers had been installed in the mid-sixties. The kitchen would be available for use downstairs and would also serve coffee and baked goods to the store's patrons. The business plan AJ had worked on all through college was nearly perfect and addressed every detail down to the letter.

AJ looked around at the dusty space and didn't see the dirt and grime. She saw pure potential. In all the beat-up and broken furniture, she saw the blessing in so many café-style tables that she could opt only keep the two tops and put the larger ones upstairs for the time being. Instead of lamenting how many rooms there were to clean up, she saw the beauty in having so many rooms so that there would be plenty of storage space.

She walked the old hotel with a pen and notepad in hand. On the notepad, she had made a list of workers she would need to hire—a cleaning crew, a foundation engineer, and a plumber. She knew some people around town who would be more than happy to work for store credit.

She'd need a lot of carpentry done with the bookshelves and all the doors that were to be removed from the first upstairs floor. Customers would need to see that those ten rooms held additional merchandise from the lobby floor. She'd have shelves that lined the hallway to make it more obvious and artsy painted signs attached to the banister across from the door to each room with the room number:

1A Business, Psychology, Self-Help

1B Sociology and Anthropology, Science, Math

1C Ancient History

1D Military History

1E Political Science, Current Non-fiction

1F Religion

1G Metaphysics, Health, Nutrition

1H Home Arts, Antiques, Collecting

1I Home Arts, Antiques, Collecting

1J Romance Novels, Children's Books, Clearance

She followed the plan in the notebook down to the letter. AJ remembered when Granddaddy Jack had decided to arrange things this way. He'd counted out all the reasons while she wrote them down in their book. First, there had to be reasons to force people into the quiet upper levels, so she'd chosen the most popular subjects (history and religion) and items (romance novels and clearance) with the highest cost of goods (antiquities) upstairs.

Everyone loves their *New York Times* bestselling fiction titles, but unless it was the latest and the greatest, they were the hardest books to move and the titles she would have most readily available. The store wasn't designed to be small children friendly, so she'd allotted the children's books the least amount of space.

Titles above a seventh-grade reading level she would mix in with the adult sections. "Age twelve, if you're shopping in a store like this on your own, is a good time to be a grownup," Granddaddy Jack had said. The home arts and collectible room took up two suites, as some rooms were joined by a door and shared a bathroom. Back in the days when wealthy families had stayed in the hotel, children could be in the room next to their parents.

AJ had planned to remove the door connecting those two rooms so people could walk with ease between the two. She had chosen that room to be connected to allow space for antiquities and arts-and-crafts vendors to keep a table on consignment in the space that was once the bathroom. These items would correspond well with the books in that section.

Tourists would buy a quilting book of their choice signed by the woman who sewed a quilt also available for purchase. There were plenty of women who would enjoy utilizing the bookshop for sewing-circle parties and book club meetings if the town were what it was when she was younger. She would remind them.

With the adjoining rooms in mind, she chose 2H & 2I to be her master suite when she moved in. It would be the first to be renovated, along with the lobby downstairs. She wanted to be out of her child-hood home as quickly as possible. Down the hall, 2B & 2C would be available for whoever she hired on as assistant manager at the store. She had just posted an ad online and in the surrounding towns' news-papers earlier that morning announcing the position. She hoped she wasn't getting ahead of herself.

Would she be able to get all of this ready in three months? That's when Nancy Harrigan's book club meetings were scheduled to begin in the garden atrium. Well, Nancy didn't know that. She didn't even have a book club yet, but AJ would make sure that happened. Grand-dad Jack would be proud of her if she pulled this off. More importantly, maybe Kevin would be proud, too. Thinking of her husband, AJ toyed with her wedding band and then quickly pushed him from her mind.

The gardens, she reminded herself and scribbled a note in the book in her hand. *Hire a landscaping crew for the gardens.*

Sam's Deli Menu

Tuesday Special: The Extreme PB&J

*Enjoy Homemade Honeyed Peanut Butter and your choice of
Strawberry Jelly (Strawberries freshly picked from Sam's Home
Garden) or Arnetta Gregor's Famous Grape Jam served on
Almond-Flecked Wheat Bread. Comes with Lemonade or Iced Tea
and your choice of Caramelized Apple Slices or a Banana.*

Nancy Harrigan

"This town is old and tired, Ms. Harrigan." AJ shifted her weight
to relieve her aching leg. "Don't you want to bring it back to life? Use
those pink suits and your position on the council to do something."

"Like what?" Nancy half-snarled. "I'm the event coordinator for
the mayor."

"No, you're the event coordinator for the town," AJ corrected.
"Spice up the events. The annual pumpkin roll isn't going to last forever if people get out of the habit of gathering. I went to a football
game last night, and no one else was there."

"But where would I start?"

"First off, get that monthly council meeting moved someplace
friendly. A place with food, like Sam's. Second, start a book club."

"A book club?"

AJ smiled and shrugged. "Why not a book club?" Then she left.

Nancy fidgeted with her pale pink fingernails after AJ left her standing in front of Abigail's Bakery alone. She'd been coming into Abigail's every Friday morning to meet Ann and Sue for breakfast tarts for years. When their boys were in football together, it was to celebrate the game day and gather treats to sell for the booster club.

They'd sort out who'd be brewing the iced tea and then pray. Then the boys graduated and married, and over time, it became what the town called the Old Widow's Club, although Sue remarried.

Nancy opened the door to Abigail's, feeling lonely for better times, for those days when Mr. Harrigan was still around, when the town was alive and well. AJ was right. This town used to have such pep. When there wasn't a football game, there were dances—not just high-school dances, but whole-town dances at the hotel when she was really young.

In addition to the Pumpkin Roll, there had been monthly rummage sales, something that had now dwindled to a half-hearted annual event. Once upon a time, there were even horseshoe tournaments on the courthouse lawn every Thursday after bingo.

These were the things that kept the town alive and the tourists flowing in on holidays. These were the things that were ultimately everyone's bread and butter. What happened to all those things? What happened to bingo? She was the mayor's event coordinator. No, she was the town's event coordinator! How had she let these things slip away?

"What is that AJ up to these days?" Sue asked when Nancy finally went inside.

"Rebuilding the hotel."

"Mmmm." The ladies nodded their heads and ate their tarts.

"You know, I've been thinking," Nancy said to the girls. "We should start a book club."

"We don't know the first thing about book clubs," Ann said. Such a naysayer. Always had been.

"We'll figure it out. It could be fun. You invite the daughters-in-law, and they could bring the girls. It could be great bonding."

"What would we read first?" Sue was adventurous and always ready for something new.

"I'll pick something to start. Oprah has a book club. Maybe we could start with something on her list."

"I don't like Oprah," the naysayer said.

Who doesn't like Oprah? Nancy wondered, but she bit her tongue. "Well, we'll pick something."

The following month, Nancy, Kat, Sue, Chloe, and Ann sat down to tarts at Abigail's and talked about *The Time Traveler's Wife.*

"Too much foul language," Ann said.

Kat rolled her eyes, and Nancy smiled a bit at her daughter-in-law before Chloe spoke up. "Oh, but Henry DeTamble is so romantic!" Chloe was Sue's daughter, and she and Kat had both known Ann their entire lives due to the friendship the three older women had always shared. They knew that Ann seemed bitter about everything and was annoying as hell, but when it came down to it, she had a good heart.

AJ popped into Abigail's to buy Danish rolls for her morning construction crew and to spy on her handiwork. She nodded to the ladies, and she smiled to herself. Nancy seemed to be holding the group together quite well. She kept them on task with reading-group questions provided in the back of the book and seemed fairly excited to be having a discussion with purpose. Soon, AJ would be able to drop a hint about the atrium and the garden.

Nancy was none too casual about peeking in on AJ as well. Later that day, she made her way into the old hotel and saw how much AJ had accomplished in just a few weeks of work as well as how much there was left to do.

"The hotel used to have such lovely gardens," Nancy said as the two women stood in the lobby area. The building was sound, and the men were working on lining the first upstairs floor with bookshelves.

"They'll be lovely again," AJ said. "I think it's important to go back to the building's roots, even though it'll have a much different function."

"What good will it do if no one will see it?"

"I'll see it. And besides, a garden is a great place for readers to enjoy."

"And discuss their purchases." Nancy seemed to be thinking aloud.

"Yes," AJ said. She looked at Nancy Harrigan with a little more than a sparkle in her eye, watching the seed she'd planted grow into a thought.

The very next day, Nancy Harrigan marched into the lobby, which was still peppered with unfinished shelves. Max Harkins was busy restoring the clerk's desk to its former glory, and a newly delivered antique cash register was waiting to be unloaded onto its new resting place.

Nancy was glowing and wore a freshly pressed pantsuit. It was pink, of course.

"We're reading *Little Women*," Nancy announced. "The girls and I, there are eight of us now—Sue, Ann, Chloe, and Kat. Charisse, Chloe's daughter, you remember her? The little bit of a thing with the strawberry hair? And Ann even got her daughter-in-law, Jill, to come. My granddaughter Fiona is in it, too, now." She said as an afterthought, "Fiona doesn't even like to read."

"That's wonderful," AJ said. "I'm glad things are going so well, and just in the second month." She tried not to sound distracted as she ignored half of Nancy's prattle.

"Indeed. Well, we're going to outgrow Abigail's soon. It's a bakery, not a meeting house." Nancy was crisp, trying to get to her point excitedly. "She only keeps those two tiny tables."

"Oh. Well, what will you do?" *Don't oversell it, AJ*, she told herself as she pushed through the French doors and stepped out onto the cobblestone patio of the atrium that led to the main garden. She heard Nancy give a little gasp—a nostalgic and longing gasp.

"I want to pay for the garden. I want to pay for the garden and be guaranteed creative license over it. And priority when it comes to booking events."

"Naturally," AJ answered. "You've such a lovely eye for gardens, and you're the town event coordinator."

Nancy eyed the girl. She had quite possibly been manipulated, and though she didn't care for being manipulated, she was too excited about the possibilities to give AJ grief about it.

"Pete's Landscaping—you know, Sue's nephew. I'm going to hire him. You think you'll have it ready soon?"

"Soon enough. I'll keep you posted."

"No need. I'll be back."

White, night-blooming jasmine had once covered the garden walls. It was why, decades ago, Nancy had chosen to have her wedding there at night. Trellises of pink and red climbing roses created a bit of a maze on the less-central corners of the patio.

The atrium pillars dripped purple wisteria. Nancy remembered standing there with her mother, wrapping white garden lights along each little vine, lighting candles where she and Richard would stand and recite their vows.

Nancy sighed, looking over the place, remembering what it had once been and imagining what it could be again. There wasn't a lot she had left in this world, but even as an old, dilapidated building, she'd cherished passing it every time she went down Main Street.

She cherished being able to look over to her left as she drove to the courthouse, peering past The Green and into the depths of the cul-de-sac and seeing that it was still there—remnants of her life, of Richard, of their wedding so long ago.

Walking the garden now with Pete as he held her wedding photos in his hand, she got a bit giddy. So did Pete. It looked as though Max Harkins had already come through and restored the cast-iron benches and repaired a few of the atrium beams. If this hotel was restored to even a fraction of the kind of establishment it previously was, people far and wide would know Pete's work.

Lavender and chamomile along the paths . . . dripping wisteria . . . and oh, the roses . . . it was a dream job.

Sam's Deli Menu

Wednesday Special: The Chicken Hummus Sandwich

White Chicken, Lettuce, Shredded Carrots, Red Peppers, Olives,
Celery, and Humus spread on your choice of either Sam's
Homemade Rye Bread or Almond-Flecked Wheat Bread. Served
with Homemade Potato Chips and either Lemonade or Iced Tea

Sam Finney

Sam Finney was a large fellow, large like a wall. He'd been a big deal on Lily Hollow High's football team ten years before Kevin Rhys hit the field. Remembered most by his peers for his football years, people were pleasantly surprised when he decided to open a deli.

He blamed Nancy Harrigan for it, though he'd never admit that. He'd grown up watching Ms. Harrigan and her ladies gather at Abigail's every Friday. Dick Harrigan had been one of his best friends growing up, and the two had always wondered where the grown men hang out.

"Large appetite means refined taste buds," he'd chuckle in response to everyone's questions about the deli, but inwardly, he'd always hoped his joint would become for men what Abigail's was for the women.

Most people hadn't thought that Sam Finney would do much with himself, so, initially, the deli was crowded out of sheer curiosity. Nice enough kid, the adults had always said, but not real bright and not a lot of talent in anything but football.

People expected him to be a handy man or an assistant coach at the school. Sam had never left the safety and comfort of Lily Hollow except for little weekend trips to small-business-owners conventions or football games. He'd opened up his own business at a fairly young age in his own small town. Everyone he knew was quite proud of his venture, and they were more than happy to eat his food.

Sam had decided to open a sandwich joint when he was nineteen. After graduating from high school with no intentions of college, he was bored. He was bored of helping his mom around the house to make up for living at home while all his other friends had left town.

He was bored of visiting his sister's family and teaching her kids football but not having a family of his own. He was bored of people not expecting him to do anything interesting and bored of people not being disappointed in him because they didn't expect anything of him to start.

He knew he was worth more than their low expectations. He knew he was capable of more than tackling guys on a field and moving heavy furniture for people around town when they were too cheap to hire professional movers.

He'd always had a knack for putting together delicious munchies out of nothing when he came home hungry from football practice, but culinary school was definitely not high on his list of interests. He started doing research and realized he should open a deli.

Sam was in his early twenties by the time he opened his deli. School was letting out for the summer, and all of Lily Hollow High came charging toward his door, scouting out what was rumored to be the next new hangout spot. Of the throngs of teenagers that flocked the deli that summer, Sam knew he owed the success of his shop to AJ and Kevin in particular.

Those two were the golden kids, especially Kevin. Where no one expected much from Sam but a solid football career, Lily Hollow expected everything out of Kevin Rhys. The town had fallen passionately in love with him—he had captivated them all, young and old. The kids wanted to be him, the adults thought he could do no wrong, and the elderly wished he would run off with their granddaughters.

It was AJ who liked Sam's Deli most, and as Kevin's girlfriend, they had brought with them a wave of patrons he hadn't anticipated. Overnight, Sam's Deli was the place to be. Those kids made his deli an all-out success, because they became the older people who haunted the shop to this day.

Sam had so much fun that first day, his face hurt from smiling as he passed out orders and took in cash. All summer, his large, red curls hung in his eyes. His mustard-smudged white apron strapped across his broad frame made him feel messy, but he was having the time of his life. At some point, Sam cut all those curls and took to slicking his waves back with mousse. Tourist season had taught him to be more orderly.

Over the years, he also upgraded the haphazard tables and chairs to soda-shop-style booths. He added an ice cream malt machine so he could sell ice cream by the cone in the summers. The deli was always sure to have large carafes of iced tea, a small coffee pot running, and soda sold by the can.

He'd tinkered back and forth with adding other food items to his menu, but mostly, people knew Sam for his glorious sandwiches. Sam even catered AJ and Kevin's afternoon outdoor wedding. Mrs. Finney hand-sewed beautiful tablecloths where platters of Sam's sandwiches were piled in tiers.

When Mrs. Finney finally retired from her job as the home economics teacher at the high school, she started running the cash register during the lunch rush and helping with more of Sam's catering ventures. If she wasn't manning the register, you could find her knitting in Sam's office.

Mrs. Finney was getting older and didn't like being at the house alone all day, and although Sam earned more than enough to have his own place, he still lived with her in the house he grew up in on Cherry Oak Blvd.

The day AJ finally made it back to Sam's Deli after being gone for so long, Sam listened patiently as she told him of Granddad Jack's plans for the property across the street. He couldn't stop watching her eyes as she struggled with missing her great grandfather and being relieved that there was work to be done that didn't have to do with funeral preparations or canceling subscriptions of things for a spouse she no longer had.

He couldn't believe that not that long ago, this woman had been the little girl ordering ice cream cones from him, hand-in-hand with his nephew's best friend. He couldn't believe that not that long ago, she was suffering in physical therapy for injuries caused during the death of that same boy. She looked perfect now, her holey jeans and boots a little muddy from tramping through the property across the street but still perfect.

The deli was slow that day, and Mrs. Finney was at Sam's sister's for the afternoon, giving AJ the freedom to spend time with a man who'd always kept a special lookout for her well-being. Sam brought her the ham-and-cheese melt on white bread and lots of tater tots that she'd ordered most as a kid, and AJ sat for hours, enjoying Sam's company.

Finally, Sam began to offer up his own ideas. "AJ, I think it's all a mighty fine idea, and don't you dare dream of skimping on the coffee or the café, because I plan to add your coffee to my menu."

"What?"

"That little pot of coffee over there? I sell one cup a day—one—to Mr. Henry for a dollar. It's not because this town doesn't want coffee, they just don't want truck-driver-diner coffee, which is all I seem to be able to manage. I've seen the market for it for some time, but I'm a sandwich man.

"You get that bookstore running with a decent coffee shop on the side, and I'll keep selling my crap coffee for a dollar, but I can add yours for three. We can serve it with the specials, and I'll have it gopher-ed on over here. Just sell it to me at cost.

"We can do the same with my sandwiches. Someone asks you for food not on your menu, we'll make it happen. Rather than send the customer across the street, take orders and we'll do all the running."

"Sam, will that work?"

"I think it might. Talk to Abigail, too. Tourist season is nice, but with your bookshop, we could make killings year round."

By AJ's grand opening, Sam planned to have worked up an extremely simple to-go menu to keep in the café at The Bookshop Hotel, featuring five of the least expensive sandwiches listed at a dollar more than they cost in the deli itself. On the bottom of the menu would be a note stating that you could order off a more extensive menu across the street at Sam's Deli.

Sam would do the same for AJ. He would serve her fancy breakfast blend coffee with any of the breakfast sandwich meals. He posted a note on the bottom of his in-store menu stating that there were more exciting coffees across the street at The Bookshop Hotel, or you could have a cup of Folgers for a dollar.

It wasn't long before AJ realized what a huge project she had on her hands and the potential it held. She was going to need help.

Sam's Deli Menu

Thursday Special: The Bacon Sub

Eight slices of Crispy Bacon, Lettuce, Fresh Spinach Leaves, Green Bell Peppers, Red Onions, Black Olives, Cucumber Slices, Tomato, Jalapeños, and Chipotle Spread on a Six-Inch Honey Wheat Sub. Served with Homemade Potato Chips and your choice of Iced Tea or Lemonade.

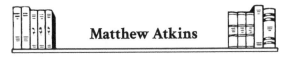

Matthew Atkins

When AJ met Matthew, she was covered in dust and dirt. The hammer in her hand rested against her snug-fitting holey jeans as she ordered four construction workers around like it was the most natural thing in the world. Matthew stood in his slacks and nice button-up shirt in the doorway of what looked like an old, run-down hotel and chuckled.

He had answered an ad in the newspaper looking for an assistant manager at a used bookstore in a quaint old town. He'd called the phone number a week ago, got a voicemail, and left a message. Hours after he'd gone to sleep that night, a return voice mail showed up on his cell thanking him for his interest in the position and offering him an interview time.

Matthew stood in the doorway for twenty minutes watching her work and bark orders. He noticed it was nearly ten, so he tossed his resume to the side and rolled up his sleeves. He was right behind her when he yelled over the noise of the hammering, "Where do you want me?"

AJ turned, looked him over, and handed him an electric screwdriver. "Those doors have to come off the hinges!" she hollered back, pointing to the doors on the other side of the first balcony. "The service elevator works," she said when she saw him glance at the men working on the half-formed stairs. Matthew nodded and went to work, making his way around the debris.

He worked hard for hours, taking the doors off, smoothing the frames with a sander, and clearing out the rooms of debris and junk until they were empty. Three o'clock came around, and a woman dressed in pink came stepping through the double doors of the lobby. AJ waved for work to cease, and the four guys rebuilding the stairway stopped and disappeared under their project.

Matthew saw them enter the garden out back from the window of the suite he was clearing. He lifted the bag of trash and loaded everything he'd gathered for the dumpster into the service elevator so he could follow everyone out.

"Nancy Harrigan, town event coordinator." The woman in pink thrust out her hand as she handed Matthew a sandwich from the local deli once he was out in the garden with the others.

"Oh, God bless Sam," AJ sighed and devoured a ham-and-cheese melt.

"Matthew Atkins." He took Nancy's hand and shook it. "Ma'am."

"I like him," Nancy said, jerking her thumb in Matthew's direction. "Enjoy lunch. Toodaloo."

"Thanks, Nancy," AJ replied between bites as the woman poked her way back into the hotel and out the front.

"AJ, I'm going to run over and check on the baby and Kelly," one of the workers said. "I'll be right back."

"Sure, take an hour."

"Thanks."

AJ gestured to Matthew to head over to some plastic lawn furniture, mismatched like it was either brought from three or four different people's homes for the day or crap she'd picked up from a yard sale for her construction crew. Apparently, it was time for an actual interview. Matthew looked down at his casual business attire, now covered in grime.

"Well, Matthew, you obviously know your way around tools and construction."

"Well, ma'am, I'm no carpenter, but I can follow instructions."

"You from the south?"

"Initially. Then I moved to the city."

"College?"

"Some."

"Talk to me." She started eating her second sandwich and listened intently.

"I went to school for international marketing, and a year into my internship at the end of my junior year of college, I realized I'd rather study literature." She laughed at that, and he continued, "Well, that pissed my parents off pretty bad, so I got cut off, and I couldn't afford school anymore. I've been doing stuff here and there to pay my bills and the few student loans I do have. I managed a coffeehouse for a year, and I'm just tired of the city."

"You plan to go back to school?"

"I take classes here and there when I can afford them. I'm twenty-six years old and finally six credit hours away from graduating, but I couldn't pass up your ad."

"Your schedule is open?"

"As open as it needs to be."

"If you want it, you're hired. And I should be able to give you the time you need to finish school come spring semester."

"I'm here."

"Sorry about your clothes."

"No biggie."

"If you come in tomorrow, I can get your paperwork ready. I can have you paid for your work today by the end of the week and start you on steady paychecks. It's not going to be much at first, but once this place is redone, your housing is taken care of if you're interested in free rent as compensation for low pay. It used to be a hotel."

She dived into the history of the place and her plans, and Matthew thought he was the luckiest guy in the world to have answered that ad. He didn't know at the time that he was the only one to answer. He finally felt convinced that his decisions up to this moment had been the right ones.

A month later, he was moving everything he owned, which wasn't much, into 2B at four in the morning. He didn't need much. The suite was fully furnished, and he'd sold half of his things when he was twenty-one years old and his parents stopped paying for anything. He could hear AJ going up and down the stairs to get to the kitchen when he was in the living room side of his apartment.

He spent an hour unboxing his books, mostly old paperbacks he'd acquired used. Other than his clothes, a lamp, a few personal items, and some toiletries, his books were pretty much all he had to his name. That was refreshing after the years spent with all the latest gadgets and technology and buying crap he didn't need.

He stood barefoot in jeans and an open flannel and took the last item out of the last box, an old picture frame. He set it on his nightstand, scratched his head, and moved it to the coffee table in front of the chaise. He stared for a minute and moved it to the mantel of the fireplace. He picked up a ratty copy of Vonnegut's *Cat's Cradle* and surveyed his new place, flicking the paperback against his hand with satisfaction. Only then did he realize how exhausted he was.

He was out as soon as he hit the sheets, accidentally leaving the fire in the fireplace burning all night. It would be a few months yet until the grand opening, but the restoration was moving along much quicker than he had anticipated. AJ was truly on a mission.

AJ surveyed the floor. More of the debris had been removed, and the crew was hauling trash away outside.

"What is all this?" Matthew asked, pointing to the stains on the wood floors.

"Animal urine?" He could tell AJ wasn't sure but felt the need to be in more control than her experience would have her be. Between the chatter from the construction crew and the handful of books and binder notes from her great grandfather that she constantly consulted, Matthew was sure she was pretty out of her depth but willing to do the work to make up for it.

He was pretty sure he was out of his depth, too, and there were a lot of late-night Youtube videos being watched repeatedly. Hammering and carpentry done but not yet ready to make things pretty by interior decorating choices, there was an obvious lapse in AJ's knowledge of getting from construction to hanging pictures.

"What do we do?" Matthew asked. His impulse was to sand it, but what did he know? He'd been a coffeehouse manager, not a hardwood floor expert.

"What does your gut tell you?" she asked. She was putting a lot of stock in his gut.

He frowned. "Sand it."

So they sanded it. By hand. The whole downstairs. It took all that day and well into the night until their shoulders were sore. They got so tired of the noise, they wore earplugs most of the time. They stopped only to eat and use the bathroom, and then they sanded some more.

At one point, Matthew looked over to see his new boss napping in a pile of sawdust. At another, AJ looked over to see her new assistant's head lolling into his own shoulder.

Finally, they swept the floor only to see that all that work had done nothing but make the stains smooth.

"How long was this building abandoned?" Matthew asked when he was awake.

"A long time."

"It saturated the wood."

"You're right. We could sand it forever . . ."

"Wouldn't do us any good."

They both sighed, and, as if on cue, Sam came in to deliver a round of sandwiches. He made the mistake of asking how they were doing, and all Matthew and AJ could do was motion to the spots. They were too hungry to speak.

"Vinegar," Sam said decisively.

They made a trip to the general store and bought large vats of vinegar. They diluted them as little as possible and drenched the stains.

Matthew grimaced at the smell. Surely this wasn't part of Jack Walters's plan. He eyed AJ as she repeatedly consulted her great grandfather's notes, trying not to show the worry in her face. From what Matthew had been privy to see, the old man had left extensively detailed plans, ledgers, and funds in a bank for this project.

AJ had sort of a "if you build it, they will come" attitude, but Matthew had done enough peering over her shoulders to see that Jack knew she'd need a little more than that. Animal urine on the floorboards, however, was not addressed in the plans.

"At least it doesn't smell like feral cat piss now," one of the crewman said as he worked on the plumbing in kitchen.

It seemed everyone in town was dropping by to see what the holdup was. Word got around fast that there were stains on the hardwood and AJ refused to cover the floors with tile or carpet.

"Damn fools," Harper Jay said, lighting his cigar while he stood on the sidewalk and peering through the large bay windows.

Ann was beside him and nodded in agreement. "Why a bookstore anyway? Everyone knows a bed-and-breakfast is the way to go out here. Those city folk flock in and can't pass up a quaint little town with antique stores. Or be useful like Sam and Abigail—people like being fed."

"Hush." Sue slapped at Ann's hand. "It's marvelous what she's doing. Surely even tourists buy books."

"Tourists will buy anything," the reverend said sagely.

"Even a pew?" Nancy teased.

The revered grunted at her and took a puff off Harper's cigar.

Nancy Harrigan shooed them all away before popping in. "Are you sure this place is going to be ready in November? You got to wow the townies so they can blab to all the holiday tourists, you know."

"We'll be ready," AJ said, but Matthew was used to her now and heard the uncertainty in her voice.

"Bleach," Nancy said. "That vinegar isn't doing it. Taking out the smell, but not the color. You need good-old-fashioned bleach."

After the second bottle of bleach, though, they gave up. There was no un-staining stained wood.

Max Harkins came in to do some work on the fireplace mantel just in time. He wrinkled his nose. "What are you doing to the wood?" He looked appalled as he inspected the flooring. "Oh no, no, no, honey. No. Get rid of those." He waved at the empty bleach bottles. "We're going to the hardware store. Now."

As they walked, Max pushing his wheelbarrow that he loaded supplies in when working away from his own garage, he explained, "You can't beat that kind of damage. That place was boarded up for years. Skunks, mice, cats, dogs, rabbits, you name it—every wild animal in Lily Hollow has peed on that wood. It soaked through the carpet and the carpet pad, then it was held in place. The wood is still good, it's just not pretty."

Matthew and AJ followed the man right into the hardware store and down a few aisles as he talked. Apparently, they did the right thing sanding it, but beyond that, they'd have to stain it. "Choose a color," Max said when they were parked in front of the wood stains with his wheel barrow.

"I like this one that says *oak*," AJ said.

"Darker. You got to cover the stains. All of them."

Matthew scratched his chin, reached out, and grabbed a nice dark one near the one AJ had chosen. "Dark Chocolate Oak," he read aloud.

AJ snickered at him, "I'm not even sure what that means, but I like it."

The grand opening was exciting and, as it turned out, just in time for the mad holiday rush. It was November 1, so the citizens of Lily Hollow were already scouting out Christmas sales, and the B&B owners were looking for local business coupons to offer their patrons.

Halloween decorations were coming down from the night before, and pumpkin seeds scattered the streets from the annual Pumpkin Roll, which was nothing more than a really messy pumpkin race through the center of town.

Matthew sat on the patio of Sam's Deli and watched it all with great interest. AJ had told him that in the past, the person to get their pumpkin to the steps of the courthouse the fastest would win a trophy, but this year, Nancy had collected items from all the local businesses and piled them up in a gift basket. AJ included a gift certificate to the bookshop and announced the grand opening of the shop at the end of the race.

A kid named Devon Henley won the race that year. He was the first person to beat Sam Finney ever. Devon was fifteen and, naturally, quite proud of himself. AJ couldn't wait to see what he thought of the shop. He was a good kid with a lot of influence over other good kids at the high school, which could make the store a lot of money in the long run.

"Those high school kids have the power to make us or break us," AJ had told Matthew, remembering how she and Kevin had affected the outcome of Sam's Deli. He believed her.

On opening day, the displays were set. AJ had collected a mountain of Thanksgiving and Christmas cookbooks that lined the walls of the café area, and Matthew had built in waist-high shelving units around the entire dining area for cookbooks and kitchen/café related items.

They were far enough away from the tables to not get destroyed by spilled coffee or overcrowd disinterested customers but close enough so that the older ladies could pick one up and browse through it. AJ planned to eventually serve certain baked goods that Abigail made especially to encourage sales for specific books. For the grand opening, though, she was serving Abigail's staple, tarts and Danishes.

The latest fantasy fad had its own table in the path between the entrance and the register counter. It was crisp and clean, towering high toward the open air under the main chandelier of the old lobby. The signs were polished, and the store was empty of dust and any remnants of debris.

There was a smell of oak and pine throughout, fresh and mingling with the coffee bean and chai tea wafting from the café. AJ had a few cinnamon and hazelnut candles burning on the register counter and in the offices.

New merchandise was lovingly branded with "The Bookshop Hotel" stickers and logos and priced neatly underneath. Used merchandise had a "used" sticker, and the "Bookshop Hotel" stamp was on the inside with a price penciled underneath. And underneath all the coffee, tea, cinnamon, and wood was the beautiful odor of ink and old books.

Matthew was poking the fire in café fireplace. It was massive, large enough for two café two-tops to be comfortably placed in front of it. It used to be the main feature of the large, carpeted hotel dining room, and AJ couldn't help but be pleased with the restoration of the mantel and how it complemented the new layout of the café.

She had placed a plaque to the right of the hearth that stated, "Lovingly restored by Max Harkins," as he had not charged her for that part of his handiwork. The main wall separating the dining room from the lobby had become a half-wall with double-sided shelving.

The carpet was gone, and the construction crew had found a hardwood floor from when the hotel actually used to be a house. Matthew had read some books on floor restoration and made it look gorgeous and new.

There was a small line under the "Grand Opening" sign outside. "Ok," AJ breathed. "Let's do this thing." People rushed in to get out of the chilly morning air, but once in, they seemed to just pick around and talk to each other. AJ realized they weren't here to shop, just to see what all the fuss was about.

AJ wouldn't panic. She picked up a tray of apple cinnamon tarts and started parading around the room, finding the people she'd known all her life and addressing them personally.

"Hello, Mrs. Finney. Have a tart. Thank you for coming. The knitting books are upstairs in that room on the right." She waved toward the home arts suite above them.

"Oh, there's an upstairs." Mrs. Finney wandered off with three tarts in hand, her plump bottom swaying as she meandered up the stairs.

She answered a compliment from an older gentleman. "Oh yes, thanks, Mr. Henry. Have a tart. We have coffee as well. My assistant

Matthew can pour you a mug. It's on the house today, but we hope you come back for more later in the week.

"Is it good coffee?" Mr. Henry asked.

"Oh, of course it's the best coffee. Matthew used to manage a coffeehouse in the city. He knows all the best secrets." AJ winked at the old man. "The history section is upstairs. I found some amazing World War II miniatures in an estate sale in Brennan last week. You'll see them on a display above the Holocaust shelf."

Matthew kept the coffee fresh and flowing, and within an hour, AJ was able to part from the center of the floor as a traffic director and actually started ringing up sales. The Percy Jackson books were gone by the end of the day, new and used.

The cookbooks were picked clean, and Mr. Henry had bought all the miniatures she'd told him about. Reverend Michaels had even spent a few hours perusing the religion section and purchased everything she had in stock on G. K. Chesterton, as she had suspected he might. AJ had done a lot of gift wrapping of children's and young adult books for Christmas gifts.

She also sold out of copies of *The Time Traveler's Wife* by Audrey Niffenegger, because that was the first book that had been discussed at Nancy Harrigan's book club, and the newest members of the club didn't want to be out of the loop. Nancy had diligently sent all the ladies into the store for a grand opening discount of ten percent off.

At the register, AJ dropped all the carbon copies of the receipts into a bucket, and that night, after cleaning up and closing down, she and Matthew crawled up to the fourth floor, where she'd set up a more personal office than the one on the main floor, and started sorting.

She had a library cataloging system on her laptop that she'd picked up for fifteen dollars at a Half Price Books in Chicago last time she was there. She set a file up for each customer. It was part of Granddaddy Jack's plan, to keep a list of what every customer had purchased and owned, to bring back the customer service level of the old days.

She entered each purchase into a ledger first, and Matthew started cataloging what was already entered into the computer. They sat shoulder-to-shoulder for hours, and around two in the morning, they were done.

"Now, when I'm out buying my used stuff, I can be specific with my purchases and have someone in mind and what I think they'd be willing to spend. I'll know that Reverend Michaels still needs *The Illustrated News Volume XXVII*, that Devon already has everything by Vonnegut but wants to start collecting Kerouac, and that Susan Rogers is still searching for an extensive book on upholstery. A lot of the same tourists return year after year for specific holidays. We can do the same for them."

"It's a good plan, but I'm beat."

"Oh, I'm sorry. And we've got to do this again tomorrow."

"Not quite, but yes." Matthew's eyes were closed. He was flat on his back on the office floor, and AJ wondered why she'd bothered buying desks for this room. He lay there quietly with his eyes closed for a few minutes, and she thought he was asleep when he startled her by saying, "We're gonna need another person."

"Give me nine months or so. I have to make sure there are enough funds. I'm almost out of my inheritance with all the renovation work we've done. Soon, we'll have to stand on our own two feet."

"Nine months. I can do that."

"Ok. Goodnight." She popped up, stacked all the paperwork on her desk, and scurried down the stairs to the suite directly below them.

Matthew got up slowly and made his way down the two half-flights and down to the end of the hall, where his own apartment sat lonely, a long walk from AJ. He closed the door behind him, not bothering to lock it. Living here, he noticed, was a lot less like being in your own apartment and more like in a college dormitory, only with thicker walls than the average dorm.

The carpets in the hallways were even red, like the dorm he'd moved his older sister into years before. It had been at one of those southern private universities trying to look Ivy League. There'd even been a baby grand piano in the lobby there.

AJ's taste was better than that. Everything looked a bit more vintage. He'd helped her restore the original 1920's chandeliers that lit the entire hall on every upstairs floor. Oddly, the floors were numbered one, two, and three, despite the fact that they were second, third, and fourth stories.

He wanted to fix that, but AJ wanted all the original room plates kept. Granddad Jack had always encouraged restoration over replacement. That was why AJ was leaving one of the downstairs offices empty. She and Matthew were going to a book-binding-and-restoration seminar in a few months, and she wanted a room set up just for repairing potential merchandise.

Matthew meant to take a shower, but he didn't even make it to getting undressed. He passed out face down in the sheets with his clothes on. They had to open again at eight o'clock and try to get the locals hooked on the morning coffee blends.

Sam's Deli Menu

Friday Special: Turkey Bell Pepper Sandwich

Thinly sliced Turkey Breast served with Sam's Special Sauce (Honey, Mustard, Miracle Whip, Cayenne, and Dill Weed) on Honeyed Wheat Bread with Green Bell Pepper and Asiago Cheese dipped in Olive Oil and Rosemary. Served with Milk and Fresh Strawberries.

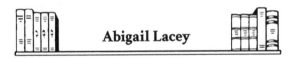

Abigail Lacey

Abigail jammed the key into the door of the bakery and, after several tries, managed to get the door open. It was crisp, cool, and four o'clock in the morning. Her arthritis was at its worst when she needed to be at her best. She started the ovens pre-heating, pulled the cool dough out of the fridge, and began working her magic.

Cinnamon rolls, Danish rolls, pastries of every kind, every morning. She worked on the tarts last, using fresh berries from her own garden first, then utilizing the gardens of her neighbors when she ran out.

Tossing dough and trays about, she almost missed seeing the figure walk down Main Street, creeping ever so quietly away from Aspen Court. *Ah*, she thought. *AJ.* AJ always crept out in the wee hours of the morning when she visited the cemetery, probably to avoid the prying eyes and the wagging tongues of Lily Hollow, and even more likely to avoid being noticed by that cute assistant manager. He was a looker, that one.

Sure enough, the bundled figure limped a tad in the morning air and hobbled right into the cemetery. On behalf of Jack, Abigail had gone to the cemetery a few times herself and given that headstone of Kevin Rhys's a piece of her mind. She knew those Rhys men well and was more than certain that after the hero worship was gone and there were no more football games to play, the truth of the matter was that Kevin Rhys had probably been a difficult man to live with. Jack hadn't had the good sense to shelter his great granddaughter from that.

Jack had been the one to lead the charge on being enthralled with Kevin Rhys. Kevin was smart and kind, not to mention his achievements, his winning smile, and his football career. The only fault anyone could find in him was his apparent knowledge of his own good looks and wit. He made a great effort to appear modest for the sake of other people's feelings, but he knew what he was and what people thought of him. He was an idol.

It was only natural that the boy further prove his perfection by not falling in love with the prettiest girl in town but the smartest, most promising one. AJ was, after all, the most likely to succeed and later became the valedictorian. At first, AJ wasn't interested. "Good girl," Abigail had said. "Good girl." But Granddaddy Jack had smiled and said, "Sweetheart, give that boy something worth playing for and go cheer him on," slapping his knee.

Poor old fool of a man. Abigail had to dry her eyes a bit when she thought of him. AJ stood at the tombstone, looking like she was willing tears to come, but Abigail didn't see any. Abigail could only speculate as to what AJ had to say to Kevin that morning.

It had been hard for Kevin to keep a job. He was never fired—people loved him too much—but often, he'd lose his motivation and passion for whatever work he was doing and just quit after moving up the ladder. His charisma kept him paid decently, but the frustration of not having roots and never being certain had worn AJ thin.

She had continued to plug away at her nine-to-five, and, a few years into their marriage, realized she and Kevin never talked anymore. They ate dinner at different times and slept in different rooms. She was lonely, he was sad. Ironically, their world imagined them to be the happiest couple alive. Everyone home in Lily Hollow was waiting for news of babies that AJ was sure she didn't want to have, not in this marriage.

She'd come home to grand announcements that they were leaving, moving here or there, in all the excitement they would grow close again, and sometime later, she would find herself in the same situation as before . . . tired.

It broke Jack's heart every time AJ called to tell him they were moving again and that it wasn't back to Lily Hollow. During football season, their email accounts would be flooded with requests to have Kevin at the homecoming game. They never went.

Every time they didn't show, a new wave of disappointment came over the town. Kevin and AJ Rhys were Lily Hollow royalty, and Lily Hollow eagerly awaited the prince and princess's return every semester. The town was devastated when the two graduated and didn't come back to live in Lily Hollow after the wedding. After being away for so long, Kevin and AJ Rhys had become Lily Hollow legends.

Jack liked the pedestal his great granddaughter had been put on. Always the novelist at heart, he thought that being a legend or being married to one meant they'd come home one day for sure. "Abby, legends always come home," he'd told Abigail while they waited. "AJ and Kevin will, too."

When AJ woke up in the hospital with nearly every bone in her body broken and the news that she was a widow at the age of twenty-five, she just sighed. She didn't have it in her to cry. She barely had it in her to start therapy, but Granddaddy Jack had called and pushed her to start again.

She was more healed than not, on crutches and in casts when she came back to help with Jack's funeral. It wasn't until after it was over and she had the plans for the bookshop in hand that she finally made her way to the headstone of her own husband.

"Oh, Kevin, I'm sorry. I'm sorry we ended like that. I miss you. The old you. You were such a beautiful boy. I'll visit from now on, I promise. I don't want you to be lonely."

Abigail had been quietly sitting on a bench near Jack's plot that first time. She'd heard it all and instantly knew what she already had known: Kevin Rhys had been a town hero, but he had also been the saddest part of AJ's life. Jack and Kevin had both left the world the same year—heartbreakers, the both of them.

The whole town had wept at both funerals, but Kevin's more so, because he was young. At Kevin's more so, because it came as such a shock. At Kevin's more so, because, well, AJ wasn't even there.

The town was happy to receive AJ when she decided to move back to town. She spent the first few months hiding out in Jack and Maude's house, where she'd grown up. Jack had always walked a fine line between losing the women in his life and being exceptionally close to them.

Fate, it seemed, preferred it that way. Though he'd been a young widower, Jack's daughter Maude had been his constant companion after she lost her own husband to the war and was left raising AJ's mother.

There was still chatter. They weren't very pleased that she was so self-sufficient, and they weren't pleased that she didn't spend her days weeping over Kevin's grave. Abigail's nephew and Kevin's father, Karl, was none too happy that his daughter-in-law had no desire to see them.

People seemed to forget that she had spent months alone in a hospital fighting for some semblance of a normal life and that she was just barely out of her first round of rehab when Jack passed.

During that time, Abigail went to visit Maude, hoping to have tea with the whole household, but Maude sat with Abigail alone that day in the kitchen. AJ was sitting outside in the garden, staring down the tomatoes Jack had left behind. "Just leave her be, Ms. Lacey. Just leave her be." Maude patted her hand firmly, not allowing her to go to the window to peek at the oldest twenty-six year old anyone had ever seen.

"She needs purpose, Maude," Abigail said that day at Maude's, misty-eyed, thinking of Jack. Jack would never stand for this. She'd known Jack her whole life. Jack and his sister climbing trees as children. Jack and his own football heroics. Jack and his serials.

They were nothing spectacular, but he'd been quite the western novelist in his day. Tourists still drove by the very house she sat in with Maude to take pictures of the house where the great Jack Walters lived and died.

Abigail remembered when Jack married his pretty little wife Emma, a girl he'd met in the city, and brought her home. Abigail remembered Jack and Emma having that pretty little baby girl, who was now sitting in front of her as withered and as old looking as herself.

Maude had married and had a baby, Sidney, and then her husband had died a soldier overseas. After that, Maude gave up any plans of leaving her father's house, and the two had raised Sidney together.

Abigail had spent hours rocking Jack's little grandbaby, Sidney, in the rocking chair, wishing it were her little grandbaby, grateful to be touching his flesh and blood. Oh, Jack. She'd loved him her whole life and never said a word. It had never been her place.

When Sidney had AJ, Jack paraded her around like a proud papa. Sidney was a mess of a girl. She never did the right thing and came home pregnant at fifteen. Still, Jack loved AJ and never let anyone say a bad word about her or her mother, who flitted around the globe like a mad woman. Jack and the town raised AJ, and AJ was the better for it.

Maude, a grandmother who lived to admit her mistakes as a mother, yielded to all of Jack's decisions. Emma hadn't lived to see all these babies, but Abigail had. Selfishly, she thought that maybe that was God throwing her a bone. Emma got to marry Jack, but Abigail got to grow old with him.

"She needs purpose," Abigail repeated.

"I don't know where she's going to find that. Daddy left her that damn building just sitting there, rotting. She's going to sit there and rot with it."

"No," Abigail said half to herself. "Maude, did AJ get anything other than the building?"

"A manila envelope she won't open. It's thick, too."

"Give it to me."

Maude never had much fight in her, so much like Emma and nothing like Jack. She came back with the envelope in hand, and Abigail tore it open, her hands aching as she lifted the metal clasp at the top. Just as she suspected, there was a notebook inside, a notebook Jack had pored over with AJ when she was young. Their dream project. AJ had always thought it was just an imagination exercise, but Abigail knew that Jack took it more seriously than that.

Abigail marched out to the garden and tossed the notebook onto the girl's lap.

"Ouch!" AJ rubbed her leg.

"Look, child. I'm sad, too. Everybody's sad. And Kevin—well, Kevin I'm sure is over it all, being that he's dead. And Jack, well, he's rolling over in his grave watching you from the heavens staring at tomatoes. Get to work."

AJ looked down at the notebook, a hint of a nostalgic smile tweaking the corners of her mouth.

"Abby, you're a genius." Jack Walters was the only human being in the world to call Abigail "Abby" until AJ came along. Abigail smiled through misty eyes, and AJ leaned on a single crutch.

That was the last AJ saw of Jack's garden tomatoes. Within weeks, she was spending all her time at the hotel, and soon, she was living there as well.

The grand opening was such a success, Abigail forgot for a moment how broken the poor girl had been. She may not need the crutches anymore, and the scars may be easier to cover, but as Abigail watched that figure hobble away from the cemetery and back to the hotel, she realized that girl wasn't cured just yet. In spite of all that, Abigail could see that AJ was doing some good to this town.

Now, Abigail placed apple pie muffins in the display window and switched the light above the display on. It blinked "Open" into the foggy dawn, and Abigail sat down to rest.

Sam's Deli Menu

Saturday Special: Sam's Favorite

Pepper Jack Cheese, Sam's Special Sauce (Honey, Mustard, Miracle Whip, Cayenne, and Dill Weed), and Thinly Sliced Turkey served on Honeyed Wheat Bread, Lightly Toasted. Comes with a large Iced Tea and Homemade Potato Chips.

The Bookshop Hotel

The building groaned, it ached, it was tired. Rafters fell, drywall crumbled. It had once been a glorious place, an establishment revered by all those who saw it and even some who didn't.

Built by a wealthy family ages ago, the house had seen love, meals, fancy parties, babies, laughter, and tears. The house had been repainted, rewired, and had a telephone installed. Then it became a hotel. Tourists came far and wide to be a part of its history, and there were more parties, weddings, and celebrities.

The garden grew over time. Each spring, new plants had been added. The trees had grown taller and wider, the roots inching their way under the foundation and floorboards. As time grew on, the house found aches and pains—a little creak here, a little creak there. Loose nails, floorboards giving the rooms voices.

One day, the people stopped coming. Boards went over the windows and doors. Everything became dusty, moist, and rusty seemingly all at once, but over a long period of time. The rodents came first—field mice first in the walls and then right out in the open, discovering that they were never disturbed.

The spiders lorded over the chandeliers and baseboards. Stray cats and dogs made beds in the fireplaces while high school kids drifted in and out at night looking for a sheltered place to drink and smoke away from the prying eyes of their parents.

The building groaned in the wind, ached under rainfall, grew tired of neglect. Then AJ came, and things began to change.

Part Two

Sam's Deli Menu

Sunday Special: The Breakfast Melt

Melted American Cheese on two Over Medium Eggs with Seared Ham between two slices of Buttered Wheat Toast. Served with Hash Browns and The Bookshop Hotel Cafe's Breakfast Blend Coffee.

"I'm a great believer in luck, and I find
the harder I work the more I have of it."

Thomas Jefferson

Matthew

It turned out AJ didn't need to wait nine months to hire another employee. Shortly after the new year, she looked over her books and discovered she had enough money set aside in the new employee fund to pay someone for twenty-five hours of work for two months. Surely someone would be interested in a small part-time gig if it came with housing.

Matthew had continued doing odd repairs here and there throughout the building on slow days, but for the most part, The Bookshop Hotel had remained surprisingly busy through the holidays and on into February. Most of the big-ticket sales were in various resale items of the antique variety rather than the book variety, but the shop never became a junk shop. AJ managed to keep it all about the books.

An antique traffic light had been the center piece for a children's display of Dr. Suess, primary colors, and introduction-to-shapes books. It had only been there for a month when some tourist drove through and paid twice what AJ had, but half of what it was actually worth.

She raffled off quilts found in old shops and garage sales, manipulating customers into buying more than they bargained for from the home arts sections. The weekly raffle became more popular than the lottery in Lily Hollow, and many people bought other quilts AJ had on display when they didn't win.

Matthew realized more and more that this tiny little blonde with a limp was more than a bookseller. She was in the event business, in the people business. She'd manipulated Nancy Harrigan into running a book club out of the shop's garden. She'd managed to set up a pretty solid café arrangement with the local deli and bakery.

She'd made friends with her longtime rival, the English teacher at the high school, as well as contacted the theatre department head, and the two educators were now hosting poetry nights together in the café. Baking competitions were at an all-time high, and Abigail had even come in and served as one of the judges, so naturally, baking books were selling like hotcakes. These small-town business owners seemed to build these relationships so easily, without a second thought.

Pete's Landscaping was continually praised as customers read the current mystery and romance novels in the garden and usually walked out with gardening books, one of Pete's business cards, and hand-crafted pottery that AJ brought in from Maggie's Pottery Store in Briar. Pete was scheduled to teach gardening classes in the garden once a month starting in the spring. The catch? Buy a gardening book of any value and book Pete to trim your hedges or mow your lawn.

AJ made everything appear seamless. It all fell into place with such little effort to outside eyes, but Matthew knew how much energy was actually put into it. And he knew they'd be hiring someone soon, so it shouldn't have surprised him when AJ came back from a trip to Briar with a dark-haired gypsy trailing behind her ready to work, but it did.

"Listen—are you breathing just a little, and calling it a life?"

Mary Oliver

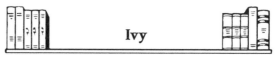

Ivy

Ivy had been living out of her car for nearly six months. The little red Volvo was extremely cliché, but it was what she had. Before that, she'd been sharing a three-bedroom apartment with nine other people. Needless to say, after two months of that, it got crowded, and she had the urge to move.

After high school, all of her friends had run off to college, and she'd simply run off. A thought occurred to her as she twirled her unwashed hair around her finger while watching a tiny woman go into the third thrift store one day. She was a gypsy.

Ivy had been following her on foot since she saw her buy a sweater at one of the shops she frequented, a sweater she'd been moments away from selecting herself. Ivy had really wanted that sweater, but the tiny lady got to it first. It didn't matter. Ivy was probably too long in the torso for it anyway. She had to be at least a head taller than the little blonde.

But before she had the chance to say anything, the little woman picked up a blanket. It was buried so far down a stack that Ivy would have missed it and couldn't imagine how she had noticed it in the first place. This woman had the eye, a gift for discovering treasure where there seemingly was none. It was one of those ugly old knit blankets that Ivy's grandmother would have made. The colors were nearly obscene. Pulled away from the pile, though, it was kind of awesome. This woman suddenly piqued Ivy's interest.

She watched the woman buzz briskly through the store, drop fifteen dollars at the register for her massive bundle of exquisite but ordinary goods, and head to the next shop. Ivy was living out of her car and spent her time haunting thrift stores and coffee shops. She was looking for something to scream out to her to change her lifestyle, but she didn't know what it was. Somehow, she imagined this crazy lady with a limp had the answer.

Four books, a box of miscellaneous junk, two lamps, and a Curious George fall-down doll later, and Ivy was hooked. She had to find out what this woman was up to. A resale shop owner? A private collector of junk?

AJ noticed the dark-haired girl stalking her through the stores, and she smirked a little bit. She knew the girl was curious but wasn't sure why. When AJ got in her car to veer away from the thrift stores and head to the neighborhood estate sales, she saw the girl climb into her own little car and continue to trail her.

AJ took a turn and followed a few estate sale signs. AJ always checked the newspapers and internet for sales. Lots of people parted with wonderful things for incredible prices at estate sales. When she pulled up to her first stop, she saw the girl was still there, parked a stop sign away.

That first stop turned out to be the jackpot. The woman of the house was moving to a retirement home in Florida and had decided to part with everything in the home she was leaving behind. "It's already furnished," she told AJ as she poked around the house. "All these framed paintings are thirty apiece." AJ looked them over. The frames alone were easily worth a hundred.

"And everything must go?" AJ asked.

"Oh yes, everything."

"I'll take ten of the paintings for fifteen each."

"Done."

"And the books?"

The woman looked behind her at a full shelf of Easton and Franklin Presses as though she'd forgotten them. There were easily two hundred books there, floor to ceiling. "My husband liked the way they looked around the fireplace."

AJ could tell they had never been read. "How much for all of them?"

"All?"

"All."

"Five hundred."

"I have four fifty cash."

"Ok. My son will load them for you."

"Thank you. It's the Jeep." AJ sat down on a kitchen chair while she counted out the bills. Her trip was over, but it had been perfectly beautiful. She couldn't have found a better deal if she had hunted for years, and this she stumbled upon almost by accident.

She rested for a minute while the woman bustled around, loading the rest of the leatherbound loot into boxes and laundry baskets. Worst case scenario, those books would sell for ten dollars apiece. Best case, depending on the title, seventy-five. She'd done well. She slipped a business card across the table with the money. Matthew had them printed just that month, too.

"The Bookshop Hotel?" the woman asked.

"Restored from The Lily Hollow Hotel." AJ didn't get a chance to say more.

"Oh, I love that place! Well, I've never been, but my parents were married there. I grew up just staring at the photos in their wedding album. I thought it was torn down or condemned now."

"No, I restored it. My great grandfather owned it. It's a bookshop now. Call me if you don't sell the rest of those paintings, or anything else for that matter. I'll drive back out and pick through what's left before you go."

"Wonderful. Thank you."

"Thank you."

She still had a hundred dollars in the console of the car that she hid from herself during big sales like this. She drove past the others on the list, popped into a garage sale on the way, and came out with a five-dollar coat rack. Peering in the rear view mirror, she saw the girl still following, so she popped onto the highway and headed home. Every few miles, AJ checked to see if the girl was still there, and she was, just chugging away in her ancient Volvo.

When AJ finally pulled into Aspen Court, she saw the girl's eyes grow wide. AJ parked around back, and the girl boldly pulled in as well.

"Can you help me carry the stuff in?" AJ asked the girl.

The girl nodded and picked up a load. Matthew poked his head out the side door and set a cinder block against it to keep it open as he helped haul boxes.

"Looks like it was a good trip," he said, eyeing the stuff and the girl.

"It really was."

"Who's this?"

"Ivy," the girl said, finally speaking. One of her dreadlocks found its way to the corner of her mouth, but she shook it free. Her hair was a mess and yet looked wildly cool. Dreadlocks, braids, curls—she seemed to have a little bit of everything spilling off her head.

"Hi, Ivy. I'm Matthew."

He didn't bother to ask where AJ had found her, and Ivy didn't bother to offer any more information. What do you say to someone in a situation like this? "Hi, I stalked your girlfriend and followed her here because I had nothing better to do," didn't sound like a promising start to any relationship.

"Picked her up in Briar," AJ announced. "I thought we could use a cashier." She looked meaningfully at Ivy who took a minute to process what was happening. This crazy lady knew she'd been stalked all day, and she was offering her a job.

"Yes!" Ivy said, nearly dropping the box on the floor when she caught a full view of the lobby-area-turned-bookshop. "I'd love to." Her heart literally skipped a beat. "It's beautiful."

"I know," AJ said. "I know."

"These are incredible!" Matthew interrupted AJ and Ivy's exchange as he carried box after box out of the jeep and into the service elevator.

"I know. I'm pretty shocked that I got such a good deal."

"I didn't think you took that much with you." He heaved another box into the elevator.

"I didn't. Got them super cheap."

"These paintings are pretty awesome, too."

"I know. I'm torn as to whether I should put them in the rooms or sell them."

"Both. I want this one in my room. We could line the stairway and tag the rest."

"Yes, good."

He set the paintings against the wall to the downstairs office.

"I only paid fifteen apiece, but we can sell them for a hundred."

"Sounds good. And the books?"

"We can start looking them up tonight. Most will go for twenty-five to fifty each. I want the lamps in the café. We could set up a display of some of the books on the mantel."

"Nice fall-down doll." Matthew plucked the little wooden Curious George out of the box.

"Oh, I forgot about that." AJ took it from his hand and headed up the stairs. When she came back, she had a little stack of Curious George books, and she placed it by the register with the doll to the side of them Vanna White style.

Matthew had everything in the service elevator by then, and he waved to Ivy to join him. "Going up," he told her.

Once on the third floor, the boxes were toted into a sorting room. Things were piled all over the place, but in an organized bit of chaos.

"What is this place?"

"The Bookshop Hotel. Didn't you know before you got here?"

"No, I sort of followed her here."

"Of course you did. She's good at getting things to fall in her lap. Were you actually looking for a job?"

"I didn't think I was, but now I totally want to be here."

"Where do you live?"

"In my car, for now." Ivy wasn't sure how he'd take this, and at first, she thought they were going to kick her out.

"Not if you decide to work here you won't."

Ivy grimaced and then smiled as Matthew opened a door to a room further down the hall. "It's a hotel," he said. "AJ lives there, and I live here."

After spending some time training Ivy on the register and showing her the ropes of the place, Ivy and Matthew processed a few boxes of the books and hung all the paintings up the massive winding staircase. That took most the day and turned out to be more exhausting than expected.

Around dinner time, Matthew cooked up some pasta in the café, and the three sat around a table and attempted a bit of small talk. When Ivy finished her food, AJ handed her the key to suite 2D and said simply, "Move in."

Matthew chewed his food slowly and watched Ivy head out the door to start gathering stuff from her car. He was excited for the business. Hiring a new employee meant they were doing well. It meant that he could get some sleep and not work nearly as hard or around the clock. AJ was great about taking advantage of lulls throughout the day to allow them to nap or relax, and it was awesome living there and not having a commute.

Sharing a kitchen with the café, they always ate fairly well. But he had turned into bookstore clerk, handyman, barista, and chef all at once. This new girl would at least ensure that he didn't have to pick up any shifts at the register, too.

Disappointment came in an unexpected wave. It meant they would no longer have these quiet dinners together, alone. It meant there was a third person upstairs sharing their hall, the employee library, and their lives.

He hadn't realized until Ivy walked through the door that afternoon that his partnership with AJ had become the most important relationship he'd ever had. These months restoring this building to its former glory in a fresh, new way had fed him, built him up, gave him a whole new outlook on the meaning of having a purpose.

Would a third person change it all?

Then again, having a third person at the shop would free him up to go take a week or two off and be somewhere else for a while. He was itching to go, to be somewhere else, even if it was just Briar for the weekend. Maybe AJ would want to take a break with him.

"It takes a huge effort to free yourself from memory."

Paulo Coelho

Matthew

For Matthew, the first few months at The Bookshop Hotel were simultaneously quiet and loud. Before the store had even opened, a working crew hung around hammering most of the day.

Matthew and AJ were silent partners. In all the banging and clamor of the renovation, he usually had earphones in, and she usually buried herself in the rhythm of a saw or screwdriver. They pointed and gestured over the noise and settled in together on the couch for a movie and hot beverage at the end of the day, if they didn't pass out first. A lot of time was spent together, but there was very little conversation.

Outside of her mannerisms, her goals for the shop, and what he heard around town, Matthew didn't really know much about his boss, yet he felt close to her. He knew how she lived, how she liked her coffee, her favorite things to eat, how long it took her to fall asleep, what stumped her, and what motivated her—without a word.

He'd only been moved in for about a week the first time he heard the thrashing and crying from down the hall. Terrified, he rushed down to her door, which was unlocked, and he poked his head inside only to get hit with a book.

"Ow!"

The crying stopped. "I'm so sorry." Her face was red, and her hands shook. Her room was a wreck, but nothing was broken. "You were probably trying to sleep."

"Not yet." He wasn't sure whether or not to enter. He barely knew her, just that she worked hard and that she was a widow. Until that moment, he hadn't imagined her to be crazy, but she looked pretty wild with anger, and she'd turned over half the furniture. Then it dawned on him. This is what grief looked like. Her eyes were puffy, and her voice a little raspy when she said, "I'll be quieter. You go to sleep."

He did the opposite. He swung the door open and started cleaning up. She just stayed on the floor and watched him pick up the nightstand and return it to its rightful place.

"I'm ok, really," she said when he was done and put his hand out to take hers.

"You can be ok and still need a change of scenery."

Suite 2A had been crammed with all the furniture that wasn't being used elsewhere and had previously made up the hotel lobby—an old circular couch, a few chaise lounges, four wingback chairs, and rolls and rolls of area rugs.

Matthew was still holding AJ's hand in his own. It was small and calloused from all the hard work around the building. The top of her head barely made it to his shoulder, and he didn't consider himself a tall man.

"I want to make this a living area," he said. "For us."

She hiccuped as she opened her mouth to answer, and he realized that she was quite possibly drunk.

AJ eyed him sheepishly. "I had wine," she said.

He started laughing, and soon, she joined him. They laughed until they both gave up on standing in the doorway, and each stumbled into their own chair. When the giggling stopped, AJ surveyed the room.

"An employee library and living room would be nice. Fix it up however you want, and we'll get some bookshelves in here. If there's ever something you want to stash for yourself but don't wish to buy, we'll just keep it in here. Like Shakespeare and Co."

She was calm again. Resolved. They sat there until she nodded off in the chair she was in, and he left her until he was certain that moving her would not wake her up. He scooped her in his arms, carried her to her room, and tucked her in bed. She was tiny and light.

When he got back to his own room he walked straight to the mantel where he'd placed a framed picture of a woman. He took the frame in his hand, stared at it a moment, and tossed it in the trash, frame and all.

The next morning, AJ woke up to a tap on her door and a throbbing headache. Matthew came in with a glass of water, a mug, and a pile of toast.

"Hangover breakfast," he said.

"You are the best assistant ever."

"Yep."

"I should thank your boss from that internship, eh?"

"I'll give you the address. Hearing how awesome I am will surely piss him off."

She offered a half-smile and guzzled the water. "What time is it?"

"Doesn't matter. It's Sunday. No work crew today."

"Thank God." She threw her head back on the pillow.

He patted her knee and left her. When he came back a few hours later, she was sleeping, so he went back to his room with a book and ate the sandwich he'd made for her. A few more weeks passed, and nothing was said of the matter, until one day around three in the morning, he heard furniture and screaming again.

The door was locked this time, but he heard glass breaking inside, so he busted the door open. The suite doors were thin, and it was easy to get past the locks. He ran to the bathroom and found her there.

The mirror was broken, glass was shattered all over the tile, and her arms were bleeding. Grabbing her arms was difficult—he was afraid to press any glass further into her skin. Her white t-shirt was splattered with blood, and he finally got ahold of her and pulled her into him.

"Stop. Stop." He was stern, and his grip was strong but gentle. He didn't know what to do with this woman. She was typically so calm, so normal, so steady. Until the middle of the night when she just . . . wasn't.

She cried for nearly an hour until she just fell asleep against him. He lowered her into the empty bath tub and brought a pillow to prop her head up and then went to the broom closet at the end of the hall by the elevator to get cleaning supplies.

He swept the glass, mopped up the blood, washed his hands, and then sat at the bathtub with the trash can and went to work plucking glass out of her arms and hands. He checked her feet for any loose pieces she might have walked on because she hadn't been wearing shoes, bandaged a nasty cut on her hand, and then scooped her up and carried her to bed.

There was a journal left open on her nightstand, and he caught a few sentence fragments referencing the shop, her marriage, Kevin, and not knowing what to do. He took his eyes off the book, feeling like an intruder. He sat down on her bed, wondering what he should do. Leaving her alone didn't seem safe. Staying there seemed inappropriate. His eyes lingered to the journal. It was open. He could read it and she'd never know. He could find out what she was thinking, what was wrong, what she expected of him. But he wouldn't. He didn't. He left the room.

AJ woke up feeling guilty. She remembered hitting the mirror and Matthew coming to the rescue, but she didn't remember where the bandage on her hand had come from.

She got up and tiptoed to the shower. It was still dark outside, and the bathroom light had been left on. Matthew had cleaned up after her, apparently. She pulled the bandage off and inspected the cut on her palm in the light. The bleeding had stopped, and Matthew had done a decent job cleaning it and putting a butterfly Band-Aid on it. She sat on the edge of the tub and turned on the water, gingerly testing the temperature.

While she waited for the water to warm up, she ran her hands over her feet. There was a tiny sliver of glass still stuck in her heel, and she pulled it out, tossing it in the tub to wash down the drain.

No more late-night bottles of wine, she thought. Wine definitely did not bring out the best in her these days. Granddaddy Jack always said they were mean drunks, but she'd never tested the theory before now. Everything she'd never had the courage to say to Kevin while he was alive seemed to come out of her once she got near the bottom of the bottle, as though she could scream him back into existence and make him be better, make him want to be the way they had been when they were younger. Make him be alive.

When they were kids, Kevin was all smiles after a football game, proud of himself, proud of her, proud of his town. No one would ever know that he was also somewhat embarrassed by all the attention and how hard he worked to not let anybody down. She remembered feeling special in knowing that. She remembered feeling special when he said, "You don't expect anything from me. I like that."

She hadn't expected anything out of him then. She didn't expect anything until she fell in love with him, and that was when it all started to change. It was the worst when it should have been the sweetest.

AJ switched on the shower and got undressed. Under the heat, she let herself relax. Sure, she was angry at Kevin—for being Kevin, for withering, for dying. But she was angrier with herself for marrying him, for letting him wither and withdraw, for not speaking up, for not understanding what he was capable of behind the wheel of a car, for not being able to admit to anyone that the car accident was Kevin's fault, and that it probably wasn't even an accident.

Her bones felt good under the water, but she looked at her hands and her puckered skin and knew she should get out. She was just wasting the utilities. Matthew might want hot water later, and they still hadn't replaced the water heater.

She dried off, wrapped her hair in a towel, and pulled her clothes on. House slippers on her feet, she took the stairwell to the kitchen and found herself face-to-face with Matthew, who had two coffee mugs in hand.

"I was coming to check on you."

"Thanks. I'm fine." She took the coffee, and he stepped back into the kitchen and leaned against the counter.

"Nice hat." He pointed at the towel. She nervously pulled it off her head and chucked it to the laundry bin they kept by the fridge for towels and aprons.

"What's in the oven?"

"Corn casserole. It's good comfort food."

"What's in it?"

"Corn, cheese, corn, cornbread, and corn."

"Sounds yummy."

"My mom used to make it when we were sad."

"Ah."

"How's the hand?"

"It's fine."

He reached out and cupped her face, tucking her wet hair behind her ear. "Good."

She looked away from him and awkwardly bit her lip. The words "I'm married" came to mind, but before she could say them, she realized that she wasn't. She looked down at her left hand, the ring still there.

When she'd woken up in the hospital, her rings had been removed. Her fingers were in splints from the accident. They had smashed into the dashboard. After the splints came off, a nurse brought the rings in and asked if she wanted help getting them on. Her right arm was still in a cast and sling.

"Just set them there." AJ pointed to the hospital tray. She stared at them for two days.

AJ didn't actually remember the car accident, but she read the accident report and saw the news. And she knew Kevin. She stared at the rings and wondered what she should do. Normally, she'd ask Kevin, but he wasn't there. Or Granddaddy Jack, but he was too sick to come to the phone.

"What do you think?" she'd asked the nurse one day.

"Excuse me, honey?" the woman had asked back.

"Never mind," AJ had said. "Never mind."

The physical therapist was a middle-aged, balding man. He had kind eyes and reminded AJ of Terry O'Quinn.

"What would you do with your rings if your wife was dead?" AJ had asked him one day.

"I don't know," he'd said. "I've never been married."

She'd nodded. Back in her room, she'd stared at them and twirled them on the tips of her fingers while watching a rerun of The Price is Right.

When she'd gone back to Lily Hollow, she had been wearing the wedding band but had tucked the engagement ring back into the box Kevin had presented it with. The days of diamonds were over, but it seemed disrespectful not to keep the band on, especially in Lily Hollow. She felt naked without it.

In the kitchen with Matthew, she was hyper-aware of that ring on her finger. The timer on the oven went off, and Matthew took the casserole out while AJ continued to stare blankly into space.

The kitchen was bright, the ring on her finger too shiny. It was a moment in time that she imagined would be imprinted in her memory forever. She was barely aware of what Matthew was doing, and at the same time, it seemed as though he was taking a year to do it. She felt goosebumps rise on her flesh, and she noticed how skinny her arms were, how thin she must look to other people.

When Kevin was alive, AJ had been small, but soft. She'd always had enough weight to be able to spare five or ten pounds if she had to—never plump, but always full and healthy. Now, despite her swollen knuckles from all the broken bones, her wedding ring hung loosely on her finger. She remembered it being snug once.

A plate was placed in front of her on the counter—hot steamy casserole cut into a perfect square. "It smells good."

"Tastes good, too," Matthew said, his mouth full. They munched for a few minutes, and when he served her a second helping, he said, "No more wine for you. I'm not cleaning up after you again."

She nodded. "That's fair."

AJ was shelving a stack of Gabriel Garcia Marquez's *Love in the Time of Cholera*. She remembered a time when she was the only person she knew who had read it. Since Oprah, she couldn't think of many people who hadn't. Even Nancy Harrigan's book club had decided to tackle it. One good thing about Oprah, she got people to read.

The first time AJ had read about the love affair of Florentino Artiza and Fermina Daza, she had been sitting in jeans and Kevin's letter jacket in the stands while the team practiced for the upcoming homecoming game. The cheerleaders had stood in their warm-ups, doing a half time routine, and she had heard the marching band in the school parking lot.

She remembered reading the line, "No please . . . forget it," while wiping tears from her cheeks. She'd stopped for a moment to look up and see Kevin call a play and throw a pass and had wondered if she'd ever be disenchanted with her own boyfriend. It had taken a long time to become enchanted with him. The idea of losing everything she felt for him had scared her.

It was that day in the Franklin Rhys Stadium behind Lily Hollow High that AJ knew she had never loved anyone else and thought that she never could love anyone but Kevin Rhys. Before, she hadn't given their relationship much thought. It was understood amongst the town, their parents, and between the couple that they would be together forever.

That day on the stadium bench, she realized that she hadn't been the one doing the choosing before, but now and forever more, she would. She chose to love Kevin as much as everyone assumed she did, and with that, she was suddenly, madly, deeply, and wholly in love.

On the way home that evening, *Love in the Time of Cholera* in one hand and Kevin's arm in the other, AJ had been extremely giddy.

"What's with you today?" Kevin had asked. "I saw you crying on the bench, and now you look like a kid at a carnival."

"We're getting married, Kevin Rhys."

He'd smiled. "I know that."

"I know, but today, *I* know that."

In The Bookshop Hotel, Kevin Rhys' widow fondled the spines and ran her hands down the Vintage Publishing logo. This is what she loved most about books. It wasn't just about the story in between the covers. It was about the stories you remember because of the story. Good book, bad book, brilliant book, or terrible, she would always remember what she was feeling or thinking the first time she experienced it.

Matthew came up behind her with a stack of Margaret George's historical fiction titles. "Thought these should go up sooner rather than later."

"Ooh, yes, these will go fast." She took *The Memoirs of Cleopatra* in her hand. "I haven't read this one yet."

"You read those?"

"I read everything."

"Of course."

She set aside the one and started alphabetizing the others into place.

"What were you thinking about?" Matthew asked, watching her front the entire shelf of G's, noticing her hands linger over Garcia.

"Kevin."

That night, Matthew snuck down to the store after Ivy and AJ had gone up to bed. He took one of every Gabriel Garcia Marquez title up to his room. Going in alphabetical order, he started with *Autumn of the Patriarch* and started reading. Throughout the first fifty pages, he couldn't stop wondering what it was about this author that reminded AJ of her dead husband.

When AJ lost her husband in the accident in Chicago, she'd completely shattered her right leg. The first time Matthew noticed was a rainy day when the cold air kept seeping through all the pores of the old hotel. She had begun to limp early in the morning and quickly feigned a headache and left him to run the store alone. He'd been surprised at the time, because he hadn't been there long, but he was afraid to ask.

Now he'd lived in Lily Hollow long enough, seen AJ disappear into the cemetery often enough, and heard enough rumors to know not to ask. He also knew there were other injuries, but noticing them had come slowly over time, not like the limp—the limp was fairly obvious to anyone who spent even just a few hours in a work environment with AJ or saw her try to trudge through cold weather.

He'd learned about the pins in her left arm from Sam one day and discovered the dimples in her skin only after knowing to look for them. Matthew knew she had broken some ribs, and he'd noticed the ridge in her nose one day when she laughed at something, realizing that she'd probably broken her nose, too. AJ never talked about the accident or the loss of her husband, but all the signs were there—the town had just chosen not to mention it around her.

Still, there weren't many places Matthew could go without hearing or reading about the legend that was Kevin Rhys. Matthew wondered just how much of the fanfare AJ was oblivious to from being there her whole life and how much she blocked out for self-preservation.

AJ sat on one of the café tables swinging the damaged leg, letting gravity pull it out of the places it seemed to compact itself into while munching her second sandwich. She spun the ring on her left finger, and Matthew wondered how long she was going to wear the damned thing. He sat a table away swallowing his Chicken Humus in large gulps.

He wanted to tell her he was sorry it hurt, but he knew better. She was proud, and she'd shut him down before the words had even passed his lips. She'd been Kevin Rhys's sweetheart for far too long in this town, and she knew how to put on a smile and a show when it was convenient for her. It was what made her so good at customer service.

"I got a family-sized bowl of the ham and dill casserole," he said.

She quickly stopped rubbing her knee, as though she had forgot he was in the room until he spoke. "Thanks. I love that stuff. Where's Ivy? She'd probably like a bite."

"She didn't work today."

"She's not upstairs?"

"No, she left this morning to go do something—been gone all day."

"Oh." Matthew noticed that she seemed uncomfortable all of a sudden. Ivy was an easy distraction tactic, normally. AJ used her for that often. Ivy was a weird sort of perky and interesting and had stories to tell that weren't about Lily Hollow or anyone from Lily Hollow. She decided to talk shop instead. "Did I tell you the home school kids are going to start meeting here for some kind of book-club-study thing?"

"No, but I know about it. Nancy came in with Melissa McGrath and Reverend Michaels the other day. They sat in the café and discussed the town calendar, curriculum and appropriate activities to coincide with the book list."

"Oh." AJ knew this had happened, she also knew Matthew had been there for it while she was upstairs fiddling with the health inventory in 1G.

Matthew handed her a fork, and she started digging into the casserole. Diced ham, potato squares, dill, and sour cream filled her mouth and momentarily took her mind off the throbbing pain in her shin and knee. She knew that when she got upstairs to her room, her whole leg would be swollen. They finished eating quietly, and Matthew took the trash to the kitchen. He came out to find her limping back toward a display to tweak the merchandise to her liking.

He walked straight to the front door, locked it, and switched the sign to "closed."

"What are you doing?"

"We're closing early."

"Why?"

"Because I'm tired of you limping around here like a hurt puppy and trying to pretend you actually think I don't notice or know. I'm taking you upstairs, and you are resting that leg for the rest of the day. We'll try again tomorrow."

"Excuse me?"

"Upstairs. Now."

"I'm—"

"The boss, and no you're not fine." He walked over to her, grabbed her good arm, and forced her to the service elevator. He knew that picking her up and just carrying her was out of the question, so he held her arm in such a way that she had no opportunity to put weight on the right side of her body.

She wouldn't make eye contact with him in the elevator, and her face stayed pinched in an expression of irritation, but once they made it to her door and he guided her to her loveseat, she began to relax. He moved the ottoman over and propped her legs up, then left the room.

Her leg was screaming, and the ache crawled up her limbs, across her ribs, up her spine, and into her skull. The pain was so great, she practically passed out from the raging headache before he returned. He put a warm mug of chamomile and spearmint tea in her hand and a compress on her head.

Her eyes stayed closed while he rolled the pant leg of her jeans up and rubbed her shin with rosemary lotion she purchased from Mac-Gregor's Nursery on a regular basis. AJ wondered how Matthew knew she had it and where she kept it.

"Thank you," she sighed.

He lightly touched her head and left the room.

She woke up the next day, alone and smelling like mint, the bitter taste of chamomile on her breath, and without pain.

"Morris liked to share the books with others. Sometimes
it was a favorite that everyone loved, and other times he
found a lonely little volume whose tale was seldom told."

William Joyce
The Fantastic Flying Books of Mr. Morris Lessmore

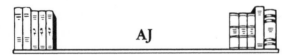

AJ

"What are you two up to now?" Ivy asked with a yawn, coming
out of the stairwell and heading straight for the coffee inside the café.
"What did I miss?" Matthew was on a ladder hanging carefully crafted
miniature books from the ceiling. He was tired from being up all night
reading and was having a hard time maintaining his balance.

The little books fluttered every time he swayed on his toes. Some
were open with the pages stiff and visible, and some were closed with
the titles beautifully embossed on the cover. They hovered in the
varying distances above the main display table where AJ had placed
stacks and stacks of William Joyce books. Up front and center was *The
Fantastic Flying Books of Mr. Morris Lessmore.*

"I love William Joyce," AJ said.

"She wanted a reason to make papier-mâché books," Matthew
teased.

Ivy just shrugged and perched herself on the stool behind the register, steaming coffee in hand. "That's a lot of work for so little merchandise," she said.

"We can use Flying Books to highlight anything," AJ said. "We're in a bookstore. I plan to keep them there awhile."

"I guess."

AJ didn't like their attitudes. She knew Ivy to be apathetic and Matthew a bit of a jester, but the two of them together reminded her too much of Kevin in his unhappy days. When Kevin was in a bad mood, he either didn't care about anything she did or he poked fun at it. She couldn't remember him being supportive about anything since high school. Everyone had wanted and expected the girlfriend of Kevin Rhys to be a cheerleader.

Kevin Rhys alone had supported her lack of interest in that endeavor. "If you don't want to, don't do it. It's not who you are." Thinking of those days helped her grasp onto the memory of him that had inspired this project in the first place, Kevin when he had happy thoughts . . . happy thoughts that came in waves as if by magic or pixie dust.

"You're like Tinker Bell with books," Kevin had told her one day. Self-consciously, she reached to touch her newly cropped hair. Feeling common and small town, she'd chopped it off into a near bob that barely fit in a ponytail. Instead of making her feel better, she just felt worse, like every comment was directed at her hair or the lack thereof.

It took her a moment before she grasped Kevin's full meaning of his comment. Kevin had a way of reminding her of the things that she didn't like about herself but somehow made her feel good about them at the same time. Kevin wasn't calling her Tinker Bell because of her hair. He was trying to pay her a compliment.

That day, they had driven to Briar to visit the bookstore. They had needed books for school, but AJ had come away with a sack of a lot more than required reading.

In the store, Kevin had gingerly held all her purchases one by one. "What's this?"

"I don't know. I'm going to find out."

"Why'd you grab it?"

"It looks happy."

"Does reading really make anyone happy?"

"Does football really make anyone happy?"

At that, he'd grown silent. It was the beginning of the solemn moods, that last year in high school. He smiled and played the hero in town, but away, he was more honest.

"Hey now." She'd picked up a copy of Blaise Pascal's *Human Happiness* and shook the book at his head. "Think happy thoughts! Think happy thoughts and fly!"

"You're like Tinker Bell with books," he'd said later in the parking lot. If it had only been that easy.

She'd felt foolish after they'd moved to Chicago, because she'd remembered how he had actually read *Human Happiness*, and the book did nothing but plunge him deeper into solemn speculation. The book had been haphazardly tossed in the dash of the car when he rammed into the guard rail. Often, in the hospital, she'd wondered if it was Kevin making some metaphorical statement. Had he planned the whole thing? Or was it one more of those weird coincidences of life?

Happy thoughts, she'd have to remind herself from now on, trying to steer back to the good parts of that memory. *Remember a happy Kevin, and then maybe it won't hurt so much that you wasted your life on a man who threw his away and almost killed you in the process. Imagine pixie dust being sprinkled around your head.* She closed her eyes and felt the burden of bad memories lift. She felt a bit of weightlessness, if only for a minute.

Before coming back to Lily Hollow, she'd sat in countless bookstores contemplating home. One day, she'd stumbled across a display of William Joyce's picture books, and, reading through one, she'd wept like a baby right there in the store.

Flying books, pixie dust, death, life, and all in between, her thoughts had all been a nonsensical jumble. But that day, reading a children's picture book, she'd found a bit of peace.

"It's supposed to make you feel freed by books," AJ said to Ivy. "A vision of weightlessness makes people feel weightless."

Matt heard the change in her voice and softened. "Of course it does. And your vision is beautiful. These are beautiful."

"Thank you."

Ivy shrugged and said, "Cool," and the day moved on. But Matthew noticed that AJ's mood remained heavy. He also noticed her caressing a few titles a little more intensely than usual.

Where Ivy flew by the seat of her pants in the bookstore like AJ had done when she was younger, choosing books seemingly at random, AJ now put heavy thought into each book and could often be found re-reading titles she had read the week before. Ivy must have noticed this, too, because as AJ was stacking copies of *East of Eden*, Ivy bothered to ask the question, "What's up with you and that book? Are you going to have sex with it?"

That actually made AJ laugh out loud, something she didn't do often. She laughed like this more and more frequently with Ivy in the shop, and Matthew often wondered if that's why she kept Ivy around. Ivy worked, but not with any real zeal. Her zeal came in planning activities to torture Nancy Harrigan, Ivy's arch nemesis, or so she liked to pretend.

"No, you little perv!" AJ shot back. "It was the first book my husband and I ever read together. We weren't married at the time. It was for school, but it was something nice that we did together." AJ remembered the picnic date clearly. Kevin had grabbed sandwiches from Sam's and headed out to the woods with a Lily Hollow Booster Club quilt. AJ had met him there. It had been one of their spots out behind Rhys stadium where Swan Lane finished its big arching curve around the town and crossed Rhys Avenue.

It didn't occur to her until after they were in college how pretentious it was that so many of the founding families had named streets after themselves. It didn't occur to her until after they were married what a toll that must have taken on Kevin's psyche, living on a street and playing football in a stadium named after his father's family. It didn't occur to her then, because there were families all over town like that. After all, she was the bastard daughter of a Carson, who lived a half mile from the Carson family estate on Carson Avenue.

At the time, it was just nice to join Kevin in the woods and read through *East of Eden* and its companion book, *Journal of a Novel*. It was nice to sit with a stack of notebooks and jot down references for their project as Kevin read aloud. He had an unexpectedly pleasant reading voice, and bits of sunlight came through the trees and shone against his eyelashes and onto the page.

Sometimes they would lie down, and her head was on his chest or in the crook of his arm. Sometimes they were opposite each other, catching glimpses of the other from across the blanket. Sometimes he laid his head in her lap while she twisted his wavy locks against her fingers. But always, for every second of the book, every discovery, every plot point, every beautiful word, they were together.

After that, they began doing all their assignments this way, and not just in the woods. When it was too cold, they would stay at each other's houses. Kevin's grades had always been great, but they improved anyway, and AJ started to fall in love with the boy she'd been dating for months.

Books were magical, and Kevin was magical to AJ when he had a book in his hands. After reading John Steinbeck, AJ didn't think her life would ever be the same. Looking back, it was the truth, not because of John Steinbeck's undeniable brilliance, but because of Kevin Rhys' undeniable magnetism. Those trips to the woods to do homework were what instigated their trips to the bookstores later. Those trips to the bookstores were what gave them the chance to bond outside of Lily Hollow.

AJ pulled herself out of her own thoughts to offer Ivy a smile. "You should read it. It's excellent." She handed Ivy *East of Eden*, and Ivy tossed the copy toward the register and said she'd take the week to look it over.

Matthew had made his way over to the café kitchen and, though listening, was setting up another batch of coffee in the French press. He did a few other odds and ends to get ready for the day as the coffee grounds steeped.

"Have you read it, Matthew?" AJ asked.

"Yes, it's pretty good." He had picked it up in college, already a fan of Steinbeck after reading *The Grapes of Wrath* in high school. He'd read *East of Eden* on a summer break one year while visiting an old girl-friend's parents' beach house in North Carolina. They hadn't been that serious, and she'd mostly ignored him and listened to music in the sun while he'd mostly ignored her and enjoyed the ocean and a good book.

She'd brought him along because her parents liked him, not because she did. They were technically still together, but she had already expressed interest in another guy, and Matthew had surprised both of them by saying, "Ok, that's cool."

He remembered her curious facial expression. "Gee, thanks, Matt. Not even a little bit of a fight?"

"Not really. I just . . . don't care."

He knew those words stung her, but not enough to apologize for them or for it to keep her from throwing away the other guy's phone number. She liked the people in her life working for her attention. He remembered her telling him this over a drink one night in a bar. They were both underage at the time, but the bartenders all knew her name, and she'd ordered him a scotch before he could protest.

It struck Matthew as funny how a book could help him remember his whole life, even the parts he'd rather forget. He wanted to make new memories with his new friends. So far, all he'd done there was partake in Ivy's little book club upstairs with the youth of Lily Hollow and attempt to snoop through AJ's memories by reading stuff she cherished. He wanted to read something for the first time with his new friends, not re-read old school books and sort through someone else's cobwebs.

"The three of us should read a book together," Matthew said.

"Isn't that pretty much all we do?" Ivy was skeptical.

"No, that's what you do at the register. The three of us together, as in the same book at the same time. We should post the big chalkboard stand up on the Green out front, lie out in the grass, eat sandwiches, and read together."

"And the chalkboard?" AJ asked, not following.

"Have Ivy draw an invitation on the board saying, 'The Bookshop Hotel will be closed for lunch. Join us on the Green for an hour of reading.' Then, actually do it, every day. It's fall, the weather is perfect for it. It would be different from the book club, because it's not about discussing the book. It's about reading the book together—the fellowship of reading."

"Sometimes, Matthew, I think you live in my head," AJ said. That was a pretty intense confession coming from AJ, and for a second, he found himself grinning like a fool. "It's done. We'll start today."

"What book?" Ivy asked.

AJ looked at the book she was shelving. "*Franny and Zooey.* I have ten copies of J.D. Salinger's little book here. We'll each take one and put five at the register. People will impulse-buy them without realizing why if we're reading them on the Green every day."

"But luxury has never appealed to me. I like simple things, books, being alone, or with somebody who understands."

Daphne Du Maurier

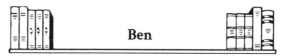

Ben

At noon, they did as they'd planned. It was cool out, so they laid a few blankets on the grass, wore sweaters, and ordered a vat of soup from Sam's. Matthew looked up at AJ periodically, who seemed unexpectedly content. He had begun to think of her as a walking contradiction—so people savvy, and yet a loner.

But here, reading outdoors, sharing a blanket and soup, she seemed like she was finally getting a bit of what she needed. If this was the kind of thing that she and Kevin had done in high school, no wonder she had run off and married him. Ivy was picking her teeth and twirling her hair, her fidgeting such a stark contrast to AJ's stillness.

Matthew was at the part where Lane kisses Franny's coat, as if it were an extension of her body, and there on The Green in the cool air and sun, all Matthew could think about was how much he would love to graze his lips past the knit collar of AJ's sweater.

At 12:45, he'd just made it to Zooey, about fifty pages in, when a car pulled into the circle drive of Aspen Court's cul-de-sac. A gentleman popped out. He saw the sign on the chalkboard in the path of the door on the sidewalk saying they'd be back at one, and he sauntered over to the blankets.

He wore spectacles. Matthew would normally refer to them as glasses, but they weren't just glasses. They were old-fashioned spectacles that scholars wore in the 1800's. Apparently, he kept books in his back pocket and radiated a nerdy chic that annoyed Matthew, because he pulled a copy of Wordsworth from his pinstriped slacks and joined the trio. He popped an unlit cigarette into his mouth.

At one, a little bell rang from AJ's cell, and she looked up. "Oh, this was lovely."

"I agree," spectacle man said. His hair was peppered gray, but he wasn't any older than AJ or Matthew.

"Benji!" AJ lunged toward him with a hug. Matthew was instantly even more annoyed with him.

"Hey, watch it. It's just Ben now."

"What are you doing here?"

"Grams said you opened this place up as a bookstore and I should come check it out. I'm checking it out."

Matthew was folding up the blankets, and Ivy had already gone inside and was positioned at her register post, still reading, from the looks of it through the glass window.

"Um, I'm sorry, Ben. This is my assistant manager—well, my partner, really." She corrected herself, trying to give Matthew the credit he deserved. "I couldn't have opened this place without him. Matthew, this is Ben. You know Sue? From Nancy's Book Club? Well, Ben is Sue's oldest grandson. He went to school with me."

Matthew just nodded politely as they all made their way into the Hotel. AJ was unusually peppy when she asked, "What have you been up to?"

"Well, I got a position last year teaching English at the community college in Briar. Not long, um, after the funeral." His voice broke a bit, more out of uncertainty than anything else.

"Which one?" AJ half smiled, trying to make light of her bad year.

"Kevin's."

"I know."

"I thought I'd see you then, but I didn't, so I came as soon as I heard you were back and turning everyone's lives upside down."

"Mmmm."

Matthew held the door for them, and the moment Ben stepped inside, all the awkward funeral talk passed as he exhaled in awe.

"Oh, AJ, it's amazing!"

"Please send your students my way. And colleagues and, well, everyone you know."

"Oh, yes, a thirty minute drive is nothing to spend a day in here. Oh my god."

"Where was this place when we were in high school, right?"

"Still here, just had a much more interesting function." He laughed out loud.

"Like you ever came here."

"Oh yeah, all the time. With Amy, actually." Ben walked the place, touching a beam here or there, thinking of when the building was an old, drafty, rotting thing where kids went to make out and tell ghost stories.

"No way, I never knew." AJ grinned a little.

"You were all wrapped up in Kevin, how could you? Man, Grams wasn't kidding when she was raving about this place."

"She raves?" AJ smiled.

"Oh yeah."

Matthew interrupted, "I can give you the tour." Anything to separate them and their mutual gushing.

"Oh yes, please do. Thanks, Matthew. I'll wait down here." Matthew was surprised that she seemed so grateful. He'd expected to be blown off, but she quickly disappeared into the downstairs office. As he gestured for Ben to follow, he realized the cool air outside may have chilled her bad leg. It hurt more when it was cold.

"This is Ivy, our cashier."

Ivy winked at Ben. "Hello, professor."

"Umm, no." Matthew led Ben away, up the customer stairs. He guided Ben through the whole building, and Ben made comments here and there about how he'd never been upstairs—the wood floors had never seemed safe—and how he was amazed how fresh the building smelled even though it looked like a lot had been salvaged. On the third floor, Matthew showed him the upstairs work room and how they all lived in the hall together in the old hotel suites.

"You've got to know her pretty well, then, living together and all." Ben became suddenly blunt outside the earshot of AJ. Now, he seemed more like a relative of Sue's.

"Sure, I guess."

"Is she ok? I mean, is she . . ."

"She's sad. Withdrawn, but she's a-ok. She's a trooper."

"You had to be to belong to Kevin Rhys," Ben said.

This was new. No one in town ever talked about AJ's husband with that tone. It was usually all reverence and awe.

Ben poked his head into Ivy's room and gestured at Ivy's mess. "That girl. Man, she's something else." When he brought his gaze back to Matthew, he saw the look on his face. "Oh, no, they've got you brainwashed, thinking he was God's gift to mankind, too, and you never even met the bastard."

"What was he like?" Matthew felt a bit of shame in asking this stranger questions about AJ's past life. Although curious, he wasn't big on prying.

"He was too good to be true," Ben said. "Everyone loved him, and every girl but AJ wanted him. And for some reason, he picked her, like it was a mission to ensure he was adored by all. He couldn't handle not being the best."

"Were you guys close?"

"Me and AJ, the best of friends, known her my whole life. Kevin, on the other hand, I don't think he was truly close to anyone. You like her, huh? How could you not? AJ deserved better than running off with the town hero. She needed someone who actually cared, who was actually heroic. I'm glad she has this place now. She needs something magical to believe in that'll actually turn out to be magical. This place is so awesome."

Matthew nodded, letting Ben carry the conversation. He imagined this was how his and AJ's friendship had been when they were young, Ben the chatterbox and AJ the quiet gal pal. He had no way of knowing that once, AJ was quite the talker and it was she who had brought Ben out of his shell.

As they headed to the employee stairwell, Ben asked, "Going all the way to the top?"

"No, it's still a junkyard up there. We're fixing it up as we go. AJ wants to open it up and maybe let it be—"

"What's taking you boys so long?" Ivy popped her head in the stairwell at the bottom and called up to them. "AJ's ordering cheesecake from Abigail's and says to get your asses down here."

"The lady beckons," Ben said, and the two men headed to the lobby.

Franny and Zooey was such a short book that by the third day of reading on The Green, not only had several of Ben's students come to join them from Briar, but a new book was in order.

"*Les Miserables* has been on my list for a while," Matthew said.

"Mmmm, no," Ivy protested. "That's like three years of lunches."

AJ let them bicker it out, glad that Ivy wasn't up for *Les Miserables*. AJ had read Hugo the last year of Kevin—not the wisest choice when your husband was on the verge of suicide, daily.

She remembered turning to volume four, *Saint Denis*, and feeling especially lonely when Kevin came home from work. He had spied her on the couch and sat down beside her.

"I'm sorry. I could do better."

She'd let him put his arms around her, and they'd sat there for a long time just holding each other. It wasn't all bad, she reminded herself. Kevin wasn't perfect, but he had been the love of her life.

Matthew offered several bulky titles to Ivy, and she kept shutting him down. "Oh my god, Matthew, we'll be here for *years*!"

"Is anyone actually planning on leaving?" He raised his voice a bit.

"Just pick a shorter book," AJ said, her patience wearing thin. She felt like a parent of two teenagers sometimes, except Matthew was her age. Matthew. She stared at him then, smug and uncharacteristically angry. He looked so frustrated. *Is he in love with Ivy?* she wondered. *Is that why he wants to read a longer book? Is he trying to pin her down?* He had been awfully quick to join her book club.

When Ivy had challenged the Nancy Harrigan book club, she'd quickly gained members, but the club never grew large. It was perfect for a little group of anarchists and revolutionaries. AJ had seen the club in session, six members sitting in a circle around a hand-tied area rug.

She mostly remembered their state of depression after reading *Crime and Punishment* and Matthew lurking in the corner of the meeting room. Lurk wasn't the right word. Matthew was observant and mostly quiet, and she liked that about him. He was in tune and good natured, not to mention handsome. So no, he never lurked. He just statuesquely occupied space.

Matthew had chuckled at the four high-school students and Ivy, whose shoulders were slumped, each with a copy of Dostoyevsky's book laying open to some Post-it, underlined quote, dog-ear, or some other book abuse.

Ivy's little club had somehow become the platform for students to air out all the feelings they couldn't share in their literature class at the risk of their grade. That's partly why the club had flourished in the spring, died in the summer, and now, come fall, would reemerge. The other part of its success was because Matthew was so supportive of it.

Now that he wanted something, AJ could tell he just wanted Ivy to go with it. After all, he'd never tried to interfere with her book club selections. After a bit more arguing, Ivy and Matthew finally settled on *The Looking Glass Wars* by Frank Beddor.

"We need fun, and this looks fun." Ivy slapped the book into Matthew's chest.

AJ had walked off, having lost interest in the conversation around the point they started to be overly stubborn. Essentially, it didn't matter what they read, as long as the three of them read it together.

"Ok, whatever," he conceded.

"Our houses are where we go to find order and certainty
against the disorder and uncertainty of the world at large.
In our houses, we're surrounded by familiar things,
familiar people. We have comforting routines."

James Morgan
If These Walls Had Ears

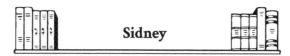

Sidney

Sidney slipped her boots back on after parking the car. The old
hotel loomed invitingly over the circle drive, a much different effect
than the building had all those years ago, the night she got pregnant.
How funny that her daughter had inherited that place of all places.

Sid could see a dark-haired girl at the register inside. She tried
to catch a glimpse of AJ, but she couldn't see past the gorgeous hunk
cleaning the windows. No wonder AJ stuck around this hole of a town.
That guy could stop traffic in Paris.

She was nervous about going inside. She'd never been a good
mother. She'd wanted to take AJ with her when she fled Lily Hollow
to go see the world, but she'd decided it would be better for a small
child to stay in a solid and stable home like Granddaddy Jack's.

When AJ was older, she just didn't want to leave. Sid had asked,
via a phone call from Australia (she couldn't go her whole life without

living in the city with which she shared a name), but by then, AJ had friends and, well, Kevin. Kevin Rhys. Sidney had nearly died when she'd heard her daughter was getting married. She'd shown up to the wedding in a purple silk she'd picked up in Bali. She'd stood near the back smoking a cigarette.

Jude Carson had made eyes at her from across the back row, both there to pretend they were better people than they were. Had they been good people—better parents—they'd be up there with the people who raised AJ. But Jude had rarely acknowledged the child, and Sidney had run away.

When Kevin died, Sidney stayed in Moscow. She was busy seeing the sights with a man named Sergei. She regretted it now, standing there in Lily Hollow. The first time you see your daughter since her wedding shouldn't be after she's already become a widow, but not being there for the funeral is even more unacceptable. She wondered if Jude had gone to the funeral or done anything. Probably not. He had a real family now, a wife and two little girls in elementary school in Seattle.

"Where's my girl?" Sidney asked. She was boisterous and over-excited, trying to mask her uneasiness.

"Excuse me?" The handsome one arched his eyebrows. He looked welcoming, and Sidney sauntered over to the café and ordered a coffee.

"AJ. Where's AJ?" Sidney repeated. "Mmmm. The coffee here smells good, almost as good as Italy."

AJ came out of the employee stairwell behind the kitchen and stood beside Matthew at the bar when Sidney launched into a story about a bistro she'd visited in the early nineties.

"Sidney?"

"Hi, baby. I heard about this shop, and I just had to come see for myself."

"How nice of you." AJ's tone was flat. Matthew had never heard her to be rude, not like that. His hand went to hers in an offer of support, lingering near hers but not touching.

"Matthew, this is my mother."

"Hi, Mrs.—"

"Nope, just Miss. I never married. Good thing, too. The luck isn't with our stock. Look at Maude. She's a widow, and AJ here is a widow. Love my girl all you want, but don't marry her!" Sidney let out a laugh.

"That's enough, Sidney. You're not funny."

"Who's Maude?" Matthew asked.

"My grandmother, her mother."

"Doesn't anyone say Mom in your family?"

"There's no one in our family worth calling Mom. Why are you here?" AJ redirected.

"I told you, I wanted to see this place."

"No, you came to gawk. Did you finally hear about the accident from wherever you were? Did you come to see this?" AJ pulled up her sleeve. Her arm had burn marks and a few scars from glass that had lodged into her flesh. There was a dimple where a pin could be found if you x-rayed her. "Or this?" She pulled up her jeans, exposing the bad leg from knee to ankle. It seemed it was in a chronic state of purplish bruising. "There. You see I was broken. I'm not anymore. Now go. You're not welcome here."

"AJ," Sidney said, her eyes sappy like a puppy's. Matthew waited for the woman to apologize. She was tiny like AJ, but a bit taller. Her hair was dark in comparison, with more than a hint of red. In the face, they were similar, but the coloring was off. AJ was so pale next to Sidney. Sidney had the sunny color of a woman who traveled and skin that was far more olive than Matthew would have guessed one of AJ's parents would be.

Her father must have been pasty. Where AJ's skin was smooth and clear, despite the broken cheek bone she'd suffered in the car accident, Sidney had fifteen years' worth of smile lines and smoke damage. "AJ, I need a place to stay. I haven't really been welcome at Maude's since you got married."

"Go find a hotel."

Sidney made a big gesture with her arms and spun in a circle.

"You've got to be kidding me." AJ rubbed her temple. "Matthew, please get her a room ready. I can't deal with this woman."

Matthew walked Sidney upstairs. He showed her to 2E, next to Ivy.

"Aw, I can't just stay in your room?" She moved to slip her arm around his waist, and he stepped aside.

"I think it's best you stay here." Matthew was a little appalled at the woman as she laughed at him.

"I'm just picking on you, kid. What's my daughter told you about me?" Sidney flipped on the light and tossed her purse on the nearest table. "Swanky suite! So what do you know?"

"Nothing."

"Nothing? Not even how horrible I am? Nothing? I might be a bad mom, but I'm not nothing."

"AJ doesn't talk a lot."

"My AJ doesn't talk? Huh." Sidney pranced around the room, peering through the curtains and checking out the furniture. "You don't talk much either, do you?"

"No ma'am, not much."

"Mmm." Sidney nodded her head. "Well, I gotta get the airport smell off my skin. I'll be down for some of that coffee of yours in the morning."

"Yes, ma'am."

When Sam Finney saw Sidney pull in, he let out a deep sigh. He'd had the biggest crush on her when he was in elementary school. She was spunky, gorgeous, and half his size as a ninth grader. He was an enormous kid—five-foot-six at age nine—and not done growing. He was a bit shy, and he thought she ruled the world.

The next morning when he opened up the deli, she was there on the cul-de-sac of Aspen Court, smoking a cigarette. She caught his gaze from the distance and gave him an exaggerated wink to be sure he'd see it, placing her finger over her lips. Then and there, she was fourteen again and he nine, saying "Shhh, Sammy," as she tucked a stolen pack of gum in his pocket at the Grocer's. Some babysitter she turned out to be. Sam was pretty sure the night Jude Carson knocked her up was the night she'd left Sam home alone watching Star Wars.

Sam remembered his mother tut-tutting over Sidney's pregnancy. She wasn't allowed to babysit him anymore, something Sam hadn't understood at the time. What was the big deal? She was a fellow mom. Shouldn't that make her an even better babysitter? Now, Sam just shook his head at the woman.

Sidney disappeared back into the building, and Sam went back to work, prepping for the day. *Ah, Sid, what are you doing?* He wanted to ask. *That girl is doing better without you. Everyone is.* All Sid ever did was wreak havoc. Granddaddy Jack had done a good thing paying for her to live abroad all those years. Then it dawned on him—Sidney was out of money now that he was dead. As far as Sam knew, Jack had left everything to AJ. *Oh Lord.*

"Good morning." Sidney sauntered to the café counter where Matthew was pouring coffee into mugs for AJ and Ivy.

"Morning, AJ's mom." Ivy took her mug to the cash register as she called over her shoulder. Sidney liked Ivy instantly. You travel the world enough, you become capable of immediately spotting yourself among strangers, and Sid loved finding herself in others. She thought it ironic that her daughter was so little like her—hated her to boot— and still seemed to surround herself with people who were just like her.

AJ disappeared into her office, leaving Sidney alone with Matthew again.

"She keeps leaving us two together. Think she's trying to tell us something?"

"That's doubtful."

Sidney waggled her eyebrows. "Just kidding, tiger."

Sam came in the door carrying a tray of goodies. "I'll be out for lunch today, so I thought I'd stock you up now."

"Awesome, thanks." Matthew gestured to the kitchen so Sam could help himself to stocking the fridge.

"Hey, Sammy-Finns." Sidney rapped the counter with her fingernails.

"Hey, Sidney."

"You know, Matthew," Sid said in between sips of coffee, "little Sammy here was the cutest kid you ever saw. Tall as a tree, too, even as a kid. I might have run off with him if he hadn't been in elementary school." She winked at Sam.

"You know, I would have run off with you, too, if you hadn't been over here getting knocked up."

"You got a mouth on you, Sam."

"Got it from my babysitter."

"Ha ha. Very funny."

Sam came back out of the kitchen and performed a Sidney-like saunter over to the woman. He leaned into her shoulder and spoke low. "AJ's doing good, but if you want anything, you come to me. She's screwed up enough without having her egg donor lurking around and moochin'. Do what you're good at and leave." Matthew heard Sam in snippets, but he saw Sidney's back go erect as she sat up taller in anger. "You got me, Sid?"

"I got you, Sam."

Sam left, and Sidney waved her hand in a good riddance gesture. "My oh my, people get their panties in a wad over my kid. I see she's got your boxers in a bunch as well."

Matthew ignored her and left the café to get started on the books that needed shelving in fiction. AJ spied him from her office and joined him.

Sidney watched the two work—silent partners. She'd never had that with anyone, been so fluid and united, had a joint purpose. He was a good kid, that Matthew. He responded to AJ's every gesture, every hint of a mood. He reminded her of a bartender she'd known once in Florida, a guy who would listen politely for days and was good natured and kind, but he didn't let anybody get away with anything. That bartender had kicked her out of his bar a time or two for being rowdy, but she respected him for it.

He reminded her of what she imagined Jude was like now that he was off with his new family, being a good person for them. Looking back, Sidney realized that when she'd run away from her babysitting job and into this old hotel with Jude that night, she was looking for him to be the better person, and that night, he just wasn't.

Matthew looked up at Sid, noticing everything, noticing being noticed. Sid dropped her gaze. He was protective of her daughter and didn't like AJ being spied on. Good. She wanted to ask him if he was sleeping with her. No, of course not, not AJ. AJ had been the good child Jack had been looking to have for so long. AJ had been a good girl, and at her wedding, Sid had overheard the groomsmen talking after the reception. AJ and Kevin had waited. That was a long time to wait, but she was proud of her little girl. For once in her life, she felt motherly. *Good for you, AJ. Good for you.*

Sidney swirled more creamer into her coffee until it turned a milky color. There it was, Jude's hair color. It was Jude who'd had milky blond hair. No one in Lily Hollow had hair like that except a Carson and AJ when she was really little. She'd outgrown it—too much of Sid came out in the end—but at first, there was no mistaking whose kid she was.

Maude had suspicions, but Sid had never confirmed them while she was pregnant. She would just shrug her shoulders when people asked. All of Lily Hollow thought Sidney was the biggest slut on earth, acting like she didn't know who her baby's daddy was. Truth was, Jude Carson was the only boy from Lily Hollow that had ever laid a hand on her, and she'd imagined herself madly in love with him.

To her knowledge, Jude hadn't laid a hand on anyone else in town either, so why wouldn't he be in love with her, too? But the Carsons came from a long line of mayors and preachers, and there are two kinds of people you don't have premarital affairs with, according to the philosophy of Maude, and those were mayors and preachers.

"What would Pastor Carson say?" Maude asked when she started to take in AJ's features. Jude's grandfather was the preacher at the First Baptist Church of Lily Hollow, and Maude remembered Sidney's diligence in church attendance before the pregnancy.

"Who cares? What's Mayor Carson going to say, ma?" Jude's father was the mayor of Lily Hollow then and had been very strict with his boys about the importance of reputation.

Maude slapped her across the face, and Sidney was Sidney, so she just laughed. It was Pastor Carson, in a good-faith effort to right his grandson's wrongs, who insisted that the name Carson be put on AJ's birth certificate when she was a toddler. Rumors in a small town couldn't be denied no matter how much Sidney tried to hide the truth, and before long, the Carson family was providing a bit of money to Maude each month for AJ's care.

But most people had already become accustomed to avoiding the subject of her last name. Even at her wedding to Kevin, the reverend had simply asked if Anna Jane would take Kevin Rhys, and no one in Lily Hollow had thought anything of it.

 "You ok?" Matthew sneaked into AJ's room, dreading what Sidney would think if she saw them in the middle of a late-night chat in AJ's suite. There wasn't an innocent thought in Sidney's brain, and that saddened him when AJ was seemingly oblivious to scandal.

"No." AJ shook her head and laughed a bit. "No one gets under my skin like my mother, not even Kevin, and he could be maddening. She has all this energy, and she expects everyone around her to want to move at her pace."

"Really? She seems tired to me."

"Really?"

"And sad."

"That's the thing. She has no right to be sad, Matthew. She's been free as a bird her whole life. No rules, no boundaries, no guilt, and no responsibilities."

"But is that a happy way to live?"

"I guess not. I just wrote her off a long time ago. Forgiveness is hard."

AJ thought back to Kevin. Forgiveness was hard, but if she could forgive Kevin for driving that car off the cliff with the two of them in it, then why couldn't she forgive Sidney? Because, broken up in the hospital and angry at her dead husband, she realized all she'd wanted was her mommy.

"Hey, hey." Matthew put his arm around her.

"What?"

"You're crying."

"That's weird." She rubbed her eyes.

Matthew laughed a little, "AJ, you can cry a little. Your husband died, the only parent you really had died, and your mom is certifiably crazy. You can cry a little."

"I know it doesn't seem like it, Matthew, but I'm feeling so much better. I really love this place. Rebuilding this hotel, it's kind of rebuilding me. And then she comes. And . . . I just wasn't ready."

"I guess we're not the ones that decide what we're ready for."

"No, we really aren't."

Sidney was gone the next day. She left a note for AJ. "I won't bother you, but if you need me, I'll be here." And for the first time in her life, AJ had a phone number she could use to reach her mother.

It was a false moment of intimacy, Matthew thought later. She was stressed because her mother was here, so she leaned on him both literally and figuratively. As soon as Sidney was gone, it was like going back to square one with AJ. She buried herself in plans, basically hid from him, or sent him on pointless errands.

Nancy Harrigan's book club berated him endlessly about plans for a Christmas celebration they wanted to have for the members and anyone who wanted to look into joining for the New Year. Sue and Ann usually came in trailing behind her. Ann was far less surly than usual, and Sue took every opportunity to point that out to Matthew.

"This place has really opened her up," Sue commented as she nodded to Ann. Matthew smiled and let her help him sort books on his cart. She was a practical woman who enjoyed having something to do. Ann, used to staring people down with cynical glares, was perched on her favorite chair in the café while Nancy laid out elegant invitations for AJ to approve. Ann wasn't exactly smiling, but she had a contented expression that would have shocked an onlooker if they had known the woman for long.

The town of Lily Hollow was becoming a family again. Every family has a fixture—a center—they revolve around and are guided by, a person or place they flock to in times of stress and joy. The bookshop had quickly become that fixture just as it had been when it was the hotel. Everyone was welcome except Sidney, and that didn't sit well with Matthew. It made him miss his own parents, his original family.

Matthew's parents were nothing like AJ's. They were kind, thoughtful people. His mom was a dutiful housewife who ran an interior decorating company from their home. She was a little artistic and a lot compromising, which was why it had come to a shock to Matthew when she had sided with his Dad in the argument about college.

Matthew's Dad was a hard-working electrical engineer. He wore suits, made a lot of money, bought his wife a large house, taught men's Sunday school classes at their church, and had been pretty stubborn about Matthew finishing college with a degree he deemed worthy. In hindsight, Matthew realized that his father's request wouldn't have been too difficult to honor.

After all, Joseph Atkins was generally a reasonable man in most other things. But when his son had chosen to serve coffee for a living after he had cut him off financially, they had stopped speaking. Joseph Atkins had expected that withholding money would force Matthew's hand, not send him running.

Matthew found out the hard way that if his father wasn't speaking to someone, neither was his mother. Barbara Atkins's husband coming first was the one thing on which she did not compromise, and come hell or high water, Matthew had to make up with his father if he ever wanted a chat with her again.

After seeing the way Sidney and AJ's relationship had just festered all these years, Matthew had to fix it. He had to see his parents and make things right. He wanted children one day, and children needed grandparents. He couldn't trust that AJ's parents would be there, and he couldn't trust that his plan would work.

I did it again, he thought. He had just imagined himself in a life with AJ—again. AJ wouldn't even let him in half the time. How was he going to marry her? It didn't matter. Setting things right with Sidney was in the best interest of the shop, and it was in the best interest of Lily Hollow. Forgiveness begets forgiveness.

He needed to get away to make any of it possible.

Matthew took in the smell of the books, the coffee, the old building, and the autumn leaves blowing in the back door from the garden.

"It's one thing to build the house you've already contracted in your head, the one you've calculated will be right for you; it's another to move into what was once someone else's dream and try to reshape it to match a vague template in your heart."

James Morgan
If These Walls Had Ears

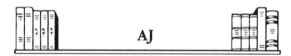

AJ

"Wine?" Matthew asked.

AJ took a sip and shook her head, "Cran-grape juice. I'm being good."

"Ah. What's that?"

AJ closed the book. "*The Secret of Lost Things*, Sheridan Hay. I like it so far."

"Mmmm."

She sat awkwardly, holding both glass and book, trying to figure out what it was that Matthew wanted from her. "Look. I'm tired, Matthew. What is it now?"

He was taken aback. "Nothing. I don't want anything, AJ." Then he left the room. AJ felt relief and then guilt, then an unexpected wave of disappointment.

She tossed the book aside and picked up another, a blue book on her nightstand called *If These Walls Had Ears*. It was a biography of a house, and she read tidbits of it when she wasn't sure how to feel. It was the kind of book that reminded her to think outside her own life, outside her own generation.

She held the book in her hands and stroked the photograph of the old house on the dust jacket. The house, like this old hotel, had such a rich and long history. Family, love, despair, loss, culture—it was a home.

Granddaddy Jack had bought the old hotel from Wilbur Bartholomew James III in 1947, the year Maude was born. As a boy, James had seen the old building constructed by his very own grandfather. He'd grown up in it, seen it turned into a hotel by his father, and done his best to keep it alive through a depression and a war.

After losing two sons in World War II, Mr. James was old and tired and happily sold the place to a young and wealthy Jack Walters, who had made his money writing popular little serials while working in the hotel as a bellhop after coming home from the war himself.

Wiltree, as they called the third Wilbur James, liked young Jack. When the newlywed said he had a baby on the way, a successful career as a novelist, and no longer wanted to work in the hotel, Wiltree offered to sell it to him instead of letting him quit.

"I'd like to retire. This would be a great place to have babies, Jacky. I know."

Jack kept it running through the fifties and sixties, and sometime in the seventies, the place sort of died. Maude closed the doors when Jack couldn't do menial maintenance on the place anymore. She was scared he'd fall off the roof while replacing shingles or trimming tree limbs. Jack spent most his time in the back room of the house he'd bought with his wife when they first got married and continued writing his hundred-and-seventy-five-page westerns. And the town started to wither.

AJ lost herself in a paint chip on her bedroom wall. Hers was the only suite that hadn't been repainted during the restoration. She liked the distressed look, and when she came to her room at night, it reminded her of the building's history and gave her the drive to wake up the next day. This place had a legacy, and she couldn't let it down.

If these walls had ears, what would they tell her?

"Matthew!" AJ got up and ran down the hall. He was standing shirtless in flannel pants, barefoot. "Oh." She looked away.

"AJ, you've seen me shirtless." He found her bashfulness humorous. She was the one who had been married before.

"Well, I had an idea."

"I'm going to bed. Get Ivy."

It was AJ's turn to be taken aback. "I . . ."

"Yes?"

"I . . ."

"You're gonna have to say it, AJ. Just spit it out."

I need you, she thought, but the words wouldn't come out. She just turned and headed up the stairwell alone.

There was so much in storage on the hotel's fourth floor. All the suites had been cleaned once through and bandaged a bit—but not quite restored—and then used for junk until further notice. Maude had wanted everything from the hotel out of the house and out of the garage.

"If you're opening up, this crap has to go. Daddy's gone. I don't have to store his memories anymore." AJ's grandmother was a hard woman, void of the typical sentiments AJ found present in other people's grandmothers. Abigail Lacey had seemed more of a grandmother to AJ all these years than Maude.

Then again, with Sidney off globetrotting, Maude had been more of a mother, or what AJ imagined mothers would be if they weren't Sidney. Sidney had always seemed like more of a distant sister or cousin who tried to fit AJ into her busy schedule once in a blue moon.

AJ had been angry at Maude for flushing Granddaddy Jack's stuff out so quickly, so urgently. Now, she was grateful. The hotel's entire history had been crammed into suite 3A. Her leg ached as she got to the last step and made her way to 3A's door. She hadn't been up there since Matthew helped her moved everything there, before Ivy had joined them. Had it really been over a year?

The room was dusty, and AJ had to swat away more than a few spider webs and bugs. She needed to make a point to have these rooms cleaned once a month. She'd ask Ivy in the morning or call Amberlee Jones's cleaning service. The door creaked behind her, and she jumped a little.

"Sorry. Didn't mean to scare you." It was Matthew. He was dressed now, looking a little less impatient than before. "What's your idea?"

"Do you remember when we were moving this stuff in here? Those boxes of guest books?"

"Yeah. I think I set them . . ." Matthew started poking his way through the stacks and piles. " . . .over here." He pulled the lid off a box.

"That would've taken me all night." AJ started making her way to the back of the suite, but Matthew held his hand up and swung the box into his arms. He carried it to the hallway and set it near the service elevator.

"That's only 1954 to '65," he said. He fished his way back into the deep. "It looks like you've got a box of '65 to closing and three or four really old boxes. Oh, and there's a whole box of just weddings."

"Bring the '65 to close and the weddings."

Matthew did as she asked, and once the boxes were in the service elevator, he asked, "So?"

"To my room." AJ could see he was frustrated with her, but she still wasn't entirely sure why.

"I want to hunt down the addresses of all the hotel's guests and invite them to the store."

"Just invite them? Or have an event."

"A gala. A huge party. I want to meet the people who made this place possible."

"It would take a lot of time to plan."

"A summer gala, next year. That would give us plenty of time. We could decorate it like a June wedding."

"A wedding, huh?" Matthew looked down at AJ's hand. The gold band there sat loose on her left ring finger.

He carried the boxes to her room, grabbed a pillow off her chaise, and leaned against the back of a chair she'd brought back after estate sale hunting in the city. She loved buying weird furniture at those sales, and in the year since they'd opened, the bookshop had more of the eclectic feel of a bookshop and less of the hotel it once was.

The café and Matthew's suite had kept the look Granddaddy Jack had loved so much, but AJ and Ivy had peppered their space with more and more of their own unique tastes, and it had spread into the store.

He liked the chair, but it seemed to remind him over and over again that AJ didn't mind change, she just minded changing for him. He eyed the ring on her finger. That ring seemed to haunt him, and it seemed to haunt her, too. Why couldn't she just take it off?

AJ had a pen and paper in hand and her laptop on the floor in front of her. She opened the 1965-to-close box first, thinking that more of these guests would still live at their old addresses, and well, frankly, be alive. She'd start there. February 3rd, 1965, Daniel and Jane Litwin, 324 Kansas St. If the city and state weren't included, did that mean they were nearby? The research began.

After the tenth entry, AJ and Matthew leaned back and sighed. They'd been at it for hours, hunting down names on every search engine they could find. Some had been easy. A few were yet to be found. AJ had a crick in her neck. Matthew had his laptop open. He had designed a beautiful invitation for the gala and was just waiting on AJ to choose official dates.

Matthew was good with a computer—he had designed all the shop's websites and managed the online sales a lot of the time. AJ didn't know how she could have done everything without him. How lucky was she that he, of all people, had answered her ad?

"What was your wedding like?" Matthew asked, not so much because he was interested, but because she never talked about it. Don't most women talk about those things? Where they had finally found their dress, the colors, the video . . . He knew that's what his mother did. AJ didn't seem to carry remnants of her wedding or even her marriage, other than her ring and the books she read.

"There were violets, lots and lots of violets. Kevin's mom loves violets. She wore a purple dress. Violets and white lilies. The lilies were hard to find, ironic for a Lily Hollow wedding, I know, but they were a tad out of season. But she really wanted accent lilies."

Matthew raised his eyebrows. She sounded like she was describing someone else's wedding, something she had observed as an attendee rather than the bride.

"What did you want?" he asked.

"Mmm?" AJ was puzzled. "What do you mean?"

"Well, in your dream wedding, what did it look like?"

"I guess I never really thought about it. A wedding isn't just about the bride. It's a marriage of two people. You can't have some kind of template wedding where you just 'insert groom here. You have to know who you're marrying and what makes them happy. Kevin wanted to make his mom happy, so I just wanted whatever Mrs. Rhys wanted."

"And if you married again?"

"It would have to be something that honored the relationship. Unique to us."

"So you'd marry again?"

"Oh I don't know. I guess I haven't really thought about it." She shifted in her position and rubbed her neck, pulling a few strands of hair around her fingers as she did so.

"AJ." He pushed the laptop aside and moved the papers to get closer to her. She leaned away from him at first, but he took her hand and pulled her whole body close. "AJ, I need to know."

His shoulder felt foreign, his build all wrong and completely different from Kevin's. But it was nice. She couldn't help but sink into his embrace. She hadn't been aware of being held since Kevin, and she couldn't remember the last time Kevin had held her.

"Matthew, I just don't know. I mean, I've only ever known myself with Kevin. I always thought I was meant for Kevin."

"Kevin's gone." Matthew just held her close, her bones poking hard into his shoulder. She was so stick-like, he thought.

She pulled away from him. "We need to pick this stuff up and get some rest."

He began to pick up their research. AJ couldn't help but look to the walls of her suite. If these walls had ears . . . if they had a mouth to speak all they'd heard, what would they say?

"I believe that there is one story in the world, and only one. . .
Humans are caught—in their lives, in their thoughts, in their
hungers and ambitions, in their avarice and cruelty, and in their
kindness and generosity too—in a net of good and evil . . . There
is no other story. A man, after he has brushed off the dust and
chips of his life, will have left only the hard, clean questions:
Was it good or was it evil? Have I done well—or ill?"

John Steinbeck
East of Eden

Kevin

AJ and Kevin had gone off to college together, eighteen, wide-
eyed, and in love. Naturally, the town of Lily Hollow imagined them
the star couple of their university.

It hadn't quite been that way. Instead, they'd become casually distant. People who bothered to know them imagined they might be a
couple, but no one really knew that for certain or took that for granted. They greeted each other casually and studied together like they had
in high school, but they were mostly just comfortable friends by the
end of their freshman year. Most days, AJ knew she would marry him,
but others, she wasn't even sure if they were together.

At a bar for a classmate's birthday party one night, Kevin walked into another room with a girl. He played pool, leaning over another girl with his hand on her hip, pretending to teach her angles. AJ wasn't certain if she felt jealousy, relief, or neglect, but she immediately turned her attention to the guy across the bar she'd been trying to ignore all night out of respect to Kevin. In the five seconds it took for them to lock eyes, her respect for Kevin and any thought of him was gone.

She felt her cheeks flush and suddenly felt hot and overwhelmed by the bar. She didn't belong here. There were too many people, it was too loud, it was too warm, and her long-sleeved shirt was too tight. She got up and walked out. She remembered it being cool outside as the door to the bar thudded closed and the air hit her face. She was finally able to take in her breath.

She heard the door crack open behind her, and there he was, that guy, with his lips on hers. He was taller than Kevin. Thinner, too. She didn't know what to do with her hands, but he didn't give her the chance to be uncertain. He boosted her up with one arm, and her feet were off the ground and her back was pressed against the cold brick.

She pulled her mouth away from his. "I . . ."

Then Kevin opened the door. "Get in the car, now."

In an instant, she was on the ground. The guy had released his grip. Kevin began to lead her to the parking lot, but the guy touched her wrist. "You alright?"

"Mmmm, yes. He's—"

"Look at me. Are you alright?" The guy looked straight into her eyes.

"She's fine. Get in the car," Kevin said again.

As they were pulling out of the parking lot, she stared at the guy still standing on the stoop, through the car window. The streetlight glinted off his head. After that night, she often wondered what the guy thought he saw in Kevin, why he was so certain that she'd rather be with him than with her boyfriend.

"Don't do that to me, AJ," Kevin said once they were on the highway.

"Likewise," she said. The girl he'd been flirting with in the bar flashed in her mind and turned her stomach.

He lifted his hand off the steering wheel where a phone number had been scrawled. He spit on his fingers and rubbed it off. "Done."

"Thanks."

That was that. It was the only time she'd kissed anyone but Kevin, and he was gone in a flash. She didn't even know his name.

Later, AJ would realize what it was that guy thought he'd seen in Kevin. It was something she would later feel to her core. Kevin loved her, true, but Kevin loved her possessively, like a favorite childhood toy he doesn't want anyone else to touch. On a day-to-day basis, if it's out of sight, then it's out of mind, but should anyone else show an interest . . . As far as Kevin was concerned, she belonged to him. Sometimes, it was a really sweet thing, but sometimes, when he was feeling especially insecure, it was a hard way to live.

He put a ring on her finger the next week, and a year later, they were married. People they knew from college were mildly surprised, but no one really cared. The town of Lily Hollow, of course, threw a party. It was their own royal romance.

It could be construed as a sad story—a loveless marriage—but it wasn't. They loved each other. Even if it was an odd sort of love, they loved each other. They would have loved each other forever, despite all Kevin's issues. Even if there were lulls in conversation every few months, she would do what she could for him, and he always did what he could for her. His ability to manage simply fluctuated in extremes.

AJ read history books and imagined that this was what arranged marriages felt like. This was why it took so long for women to fight for the right to choose, because it wasn't awful. Sometimes, it got lonely, but it was always mostly comfortable, and some days, it was even pleasant. He never cheated on her, and even if it wasn't romance novel or Hollywood worthy, they had good sex. Sex was how they got through the lulls and the monotony.

She was half asleep when she was remembering all this, and the memories came to her in a haze, like a dream. There was a tap on the door, and then Matthew opened it carrying coffee.

"You slept in."

"Oh, I'm so sorry."

"It's ok." He sat on the edge of her bed and handed her a mug. "Ivy's downstairs, we're fine. Take your time."

"I was up late getting shipments for the week ready."

"I know. I already dropped them off at the post office."

Online sales were what kept the store running when the citizens of Lily Hollow seemed to already own everything. Usually, the middle of the month when the book clubs were set until a meeting, the school kids were in the middle of a unit, and tourists weren't touring was when those online sales came in handy.

"What were you dreaming about?"

"Excuse me?"

"You had this look on your face when I came in, and you're typically pretty expressionless. I felt like I interrupted something."

AJ laughed a little. "I was kissing."

"Your husband."

AJ laughed a little louder this time, ashamed. "No, actually. Not my husband."

Matthew's eyebrows rose as he took a bit of coffee. "Naughty, AJ."

Abigail

It wasn't long after that when Matthew left in the middle of the night. He didn't want the ladies at Abigail's to start gabbing around town, although he couldn't keep Abigail from seeing him. The middle of the night for normal people was already morning for a baker.

Abigail watched the man leave out the side door in the distance and sighed, but she kept her thoughts to herself. AJ and that young man were probably having a lovers' quarrel and didn't even know it. Abigail spied the boy throwing a suitcase in the car and admired his strong arms. Jack's had looked like that once, before he grew old like she was now, before he withered away.

Christmas would be here in two weeks. What a shame he was leaving now. AJ would need him most during the holidays. Or maybe she wouldn't. What did Abigail know about anything anymore? The older she got, the more she realized she didn't know as much as she ever thought she did, not about her life or anyone else's.

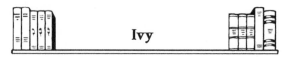

Ivy

"Where's the coffee? Where's—oh my god, where's Matthew?" Ivy went from groggy and confused to nearly hysterical.

"He left last night."

"Is he coming back?" Ivy's eyes were wide. AJ just shrugged. "I don't know."

"How can you not know? What happened?" Ivy took AJ by the shoulders.

"He came to my room, said he needed a break or vacation or something. I was kind of sleepy. I assumed he meant, like, for the weekend or something. I just told him to go."

"Oh, AJ." Ivy let go. "This is bad. This is really bad."

"Why? He's just going somewhere. He'll be back."

"You don't know that."

"I guess I don't."

"Oh, AJ. How could you let him?"

"What am I supposed to do? Barricade the man in his room in the middle of the night?"

"No, just take that damn ring off your finger and open your eyes!"

"Excuse me?"

In all her dramatic flurry, Ivy flung her arms up in the air. "He's in love with you, you idiot!"

"Oh."

When a few days had gone by with no word from Matthew and no lattes or cappuccinos in the café, AJ began to buy into Ivy's hysteria. What if he didn't come back? What had she done? What had she missed?

"I can't believe he just left! After all that research and planning the gala and he didn't even let me know—not once—that he wouldn't be here next June. And the Christmas party is coming. He didn't tell me he'd be gone for that. Ivy, what if he never comes back?"

"Then I'd say you blew it, sister."

AJ looked around the shop. This old hotel, this place, this was something stationary she could grab onto in times of trouble, a physical reminder of her foundation. It seemed everyone and everything else in life had a way of leaving, but this place stood firm.

Even Matthew—reliable, sturdy, strong Matthew—had left. She couldn't fault him for that. She could only blame herself for taking him for granted, expecting too much and offering too little, for doing to him what Kevin had always done to her.

"AJ, snap out of it. You've still got me."

"You're a gypsy. You've got one foot out the door every day."

"Not anymore. I'm a Lilyhollowan now."

"Sounds like something out of a Jonathan Swift adventure." AJ smiled weakly.

> "Reading gives us someplace to go
> when we have to stay where we are."
>
> *Mason Cooley*

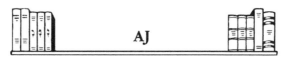

AJ

A few days into Matthew's absence, AJ curled up with Geraldine Brooks's *March*. The winter months were for the likes of Charles Dickens, Tolstoy, and Louisa May Alcott. AJ couldn't remember a Christmas when Alcott hadn't been on the reading menu in some capacity. *Little Women, Jo's Boys, Little Men, The Inheritance*.

Half a dozen Christmases in a row, she'd re-read *A Whisper in the Dark* and followed up with *Little Women* again. So it wasn't too much of a stretch to sit down with a hot mug, the snow a half step away from falling, and devour *March* after Ivy had shut down the shop below.

AJ didn't realize it yet, but the place seemed empty without Matthew, and she was just looking for a familiar man in her life to spend a cozy night by the fire with. A hundred pages in, AJ stopped reading and leaned back in her chair. This wasn't her familiar man, this was someone else's.

Brooks had written an excellent fictionalized biography of Bronson Alcott, which made sense since Louisa May Alcott had based the March family in *Little Women* on her own family. But seeing behind the veil of Alcott's imagination, AJ's own ideas of the characters of Marmee and Mr. March were shattered.

She had wanted to sit by the fire and enjoy the company of characters she thought she knew, people who had been pillars of strength in her own childhood. She hadn't wanted to have people she thought she knew twisted into something else. AJ longed for the magical image she'd had of them before reading this adaptation, but now, she couldn't think of them outside the tainted stain of Brooks' version of their lives.

Why hadn't Brooks named her characters something else so not to spoil the saintly stature of Marmee and the sweet strength of Mr. March?

AJ imagined this would be how people would feel if they ever knew what Kevin was really like, how he was just a man, and oftentimes a very sad man. That was why she rarely spoke of him, rarely spoke of their wedding and how she stood at the altar trying to find the boy she once knew in his eyes as she said, "I do." She was afraid she'd slip up and spoil the dream that Lily Hollow had imagined they'd lived.

Matthew was the only safe one to talk to, but talking to him about Kevin seemed too wrong. She loved that Matthew hadn't know her with Kevin, and bringing Kevin up in conversation just reminded her that she was supposed to still feel sad.

She liked that there was no expectation with Matthew, no expectation for her to behave like Mrs. Kevin Rhys. Matthew didn't stare just past her at the void that was Kevin's ghost. All that Lily Hollow knew of AJ was that she was an illegitimate child and that Kevin wasn't far behind. When Matthew saw AJ coming, he just saw AJ.

She was done feeling guilty about forgetting to feel sad. The truth was, she wasn't really that sad anymore. She'd moved on. She loved this hotel. She loved that Granddaddy Jack had thought to give it to her. She loved what she'd done with the place. She loved her new life, her new self, and her new friends.

AJ missed her new friend desperately. She missed his smile, his laugh, his jokes, and his desire to read anything she had read. She missed his passion for the bookstore, his ability to make the most delicious latte this side of the universe, and his gorgeous eyes. She missed his half-opened shirt and late-night chats. She missed him. He was a dear friend, and dear friends—she had discovered—were hard to come by.

AJ looked down at her lap. Her left hand lay over her half-finished book. Her wedding ring glared at her.

She slipped it off her finger and glared back. "You," she thought. "You're done." The small band lay in her palm, a symbol of the life she was ready to leave behind. "Goodbye, Kevin," she said aloud and stood up. She walked to her nightstand, opened the top drawer, and unceremoniously threw it in among the ink pens, safety pins, and small packages of tissues.

She picked up her phone and hesitated. Her texting with Matthew had previously only been about supply runs and to-do lists. But now, they weren't just partners running a business anymore—they were friends.

"When are you coming home?" she sent.

"Soon," he replied immediately.

Part Three

"I never saw a prettier house in all my life, Will.
It looks like a slice of Heaven."

the first Mrs. Wilbur Bartholomew James

The Bookshop Hotel

The hotel took a deep breath. Like an old woman after a day at the spa, it felt refreshed. Clean rooms, freshly painted walls, the pitter patter of human feet in the corridors and stairwells. The elevator was greased, primed, and in working order, and the sunlight came in through brand-new window panes. For so long, the building had longed for heavy hearts to grow light and for weary souls to find laughter.

The first Wilbur had been a jolly man, excited about building something from scratch with his own hands. The very wood contained his blood, sweat, and laughter. Will enjoyed every moment, every nail, every splinter, every headache. Indoor plumbing had been added when Wilbur Bartholomew James Jr., or Bartie, took over the place. He'd been a solemn son, not jovial at all. The building had longed for its creator, but it took the new generation with stride.

Just as so much had changed for the James Estate over the years, Aspen Court had gone through transformations as well. Hedges had come and gone, new trees sprouted up, and old trees became diseased or were chopped down for firewood. The James children had grown up with a playhouse on The Green of the unpaved cul-de-sac in the days when the family still owned horses and a carriage despite the existence of the motorcar.

The old building began to notice the loss of its neighbors. Servants' cottages had been torn down or turned into sheds. The Clements House on the left had served for extra rooms and dining areas during the hotel years but caught fire during a party and was completely destroyed. The Simmons House on the right hadn't survived the depression. Now, all that remained of the space they once held were young trees and an overgrown meadow.

Now, 32 Aspen Court didn't feel the pang of loneliness so harshly. It was inhabited and surround by people every day. The whole cul-de-sac felt less lonely, and the building less lonely in it. There was no longer a sag to the rafters and support beams. The chimneys stood tall and proud, no longer hidden by the trees around them.

There were still some aches and pains here and there—a mouse hole yet to be discovered, a leak in the pipes that would later be a source of some minor grief, but nothing that couldn't be dealt with in time.

"It's easy to mope around like a slug. Happiness takes work!"

Gemma Lacey, Abigail's mother

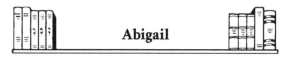

Abigail

Abigail stood in the shop's lobby. AJ had placed a huge tree that managed to reach all the way up into the second floor balcony level. She had to go shop the history section just to see the angel perched on top. The tree was covered in glass icicles, miniature brass bells, white lights, and, of course, antique books bound and hung with red ribbons. It was quite a sight.

The whole shop was quite a sight, actually. Ivy stood at the door, greeting each of the Bibliophiles of Britain, a name given to Nancy's book club for their Christmas celebration only. "Welcome to Harrigan Hall, ladies and gents." Abigail saw Nancy blush with the pleasure of having the shop named after her for a night.

Of course, Matthew was still nowhere to be found. Abigail kept her eye on AJ, who was wearing long skirts, a tailored jacket, and a plumed hat like the other members. It was an evening of Brits in the Victorian age, surrounded by the musty smell of books, aged candles, coffee, and cider.

Abigail tisked under her breath. He should come back for this. She really liked that boy, and it was no longer because he wasn't Kevin

Rhys. She'd found she had quite forgiven Kevin, a silly nonsense to be mad at the boy to begin with. It was the town that put pressure on him. The town had wanted him to be their Savior, and—Abigail tisked under her breath at herself—they had had no business doing that. So what if he left home? So what if he didn't live up to his potential? Who doesn't go away at some point? Who does everything they could in this life?

Abigail admired the room and all the people in costume eating her lemon scones. She sipped British-style tea and thought that everyone seemed sort of happy. Even AJ, who looked a little naked without Matthew at her side, had an air of peace about her.

Nancy ushered the group to the café, it was too crisp and cold outside to linger in the gardens longer than a few minutes at a time. The group was chatty and referred to each other as Lady Sue and Duchess Chloe, and even the husbands had come along wearing top hats and chuckled as they smoked pipes and called each other sir. They pulled out copies of their books and chattered about British literature, the finer merits of each title they had read or were familiar with, and sipped hot drinks.

"This is my favorite time of the year," Abigail said to no one in particular.

"This is my favorite time of the month," Lady Harrigan said.

Ivy laughed out loud, smiled at both women, and said, "Eh, it's alright. You know, Nancy, if you ever want to join the *other* book club . . ."

"Maybe, Ivy. Just maybe."

Both ladies thought it was lovely to be a part of clubs that actually read the book. Abigail just thought it was lovely that they were getting along so nicely.

"Bless me Father, for I have sinned just looking at that boy!"

Theresa Vann, seventy-year member of St. Jude's Catholic Church in Lily Hollow during confession after the first time she saw Matthew

Matthew

When Matthew had planned to go home to his parents, he expected the worst. He took pains to ensure his flight would arrive when his dad would be home, so as to not put his mother in an uncomfortable position.

He spent fifteen minutes just sitting in the taxi staring at the house where he grew up. It had been a few years. Everything looked the same but strange to him at the same time.

The Saint Augustine grass that was cut evenly across the yard looked rough after being away from Texas for so long. His mother's azaleas were oddly green as they filled the garden in the center of the yard near the Rose of Sharon that shouldn't have been heavy with blooms this time of year. He forgot how warm it could be in Texas, even in mid-December, and he pulled at the collar of the sweater he was wearing.

"You getting out or what?" the driver asked.

Matthew paid him and stepped out. His duffel bag was his only luggage, and he threw it over his shoulder.

Up the sidewalk and at the front door, he could hear Humphrey barking inside. Humphrey was an old beagle mix they'd had since he was a kid, and until Matthew heard his howling, he didn't realize he'd expected the dog to have died in the years that had passed.

"Someone's at the door!" he heard his mother call and the deadbolt turn.

The heavy wooden door creaked open, and Mr. and Mrs. Atkins stood together in the foyer, Humphrey slowly loping his way toward their feet from the living room.

"Oh, Matthew!" Tears welled up in his mother's eyes.

"Mom, Dad," he said. They all stared at each other for a minute, then everyone broke out talking all at once. His dad gave him a huge hug, the dog rubbed himself against his pant leg, and his mother stood happily sobbing.

Matthew was overwhelmed at the show of emotion after spending so much time in the Hotel with AJ, where so much was always left unsaid.

At dinner, they caught up on what his life had become. His parents didn't have much news—a cousin had married, there were a lot of new babies at church, and so on. They were pretty much as he had left them. But Matthew had so much to share.

He showed them pictures of the shop. His father was amazed that Matthew had such a pivotal role in the renovation. He told them he had just registered for online classes for the spring semester and planned to go ahead and finish his degree now that he knew what he was going to be using it for.

"I plan to do this forever, Dad."

"Renovation?"

"No, The Bookshop Hotel. It's home to me now. It's what I want my life to be."

He glossed over AJ. There was nothing to tell them as long as she was hung up on Kevin. The fact that they were being supportive about the hotel was a start.

After a few days, he kissed them goodbye. They promised to come see him soon. At the end of the visit, heading toward the taxi parked at the curb, he felt ready to start on his real mission.

The phone rang so many times, he thought she'd never answer.

"Hello?"

"Sidney."

"Yes, who is this?"

"It's Matthew. Where are you?"

Sidney rolled out of bed to the knocking at the door. It was late in the day, and housekeeping had already come by twice. "You can just skip me today already!" Sidney shouted at the unopened door.

"Sidney, it's me, Matthew," said the voice on the other side.

Ugh. What did he want? She'd told him where she was on the phone, but she'd done it so AJ would know, not so he'd come looking for her.

"What?" she asked, more as an announcement of her irritation with his presence than as a question. "What?" she repeated as she opened the door.

"Get dressed. Pack. Come back to Lily Hollow with me."

"So eloquent."

"So classy." He nodded at her disheveled pajamas and messy hair, but he was clearly referring to her attitude. He didn't like her, but she liked that he didn't put up with her bad behavior either.

"You must like her a lot if you came all the way to get me when she asked." Sidney changed clothes right there in front of him, but when she took a peek through the thin material of her shirt over her head, she saw that he had turned his back, making a show of inspecting the hallway.

"She didn't ask. She doesn't know I'm here."

"Mmmm. So why should I come with you?"

"Because I told you to."

"Do all Texan men boss their girlfriend's mothers around like cattle?"

"AJ's not my girlfriend." He turned and faced her, saw she was decent, and marched into the room to grab her suitcase.

Matthew waited behind AJ's Mom in the hotel lobby, an average sort of place right outside of Raleigh. He didn't know what had brought her here other than her desire to be elsewhere and frankly he didn't really care. He didn't suppose AJ much cared where her mother was either, just where she wasn't.

It was cold, and he wore the one nice thing he'd kept from his old life, a leather jacket that kept Sidney from referring to him as cowboy for the time being.

"Ok, all done," she said and headed to the door, slinging her purse over her shoulder.

Matthew wondered if, in another time or another life, AJ would have had more of this woman's self-centered attributes. In the same thought, he daydreamed what AJ's response would be when she saw that he came back with the person he knew she wanted to see most.

Knowing AJ, she'd give her slightly blank stare of surprise, mentally adjust to the situation as she processed it all, and continue with whatever it was she was doing. A day or two after, she might think to say thank you. Asking for more would be to ask her to change who she was.

"So, what's the hurry?" Sidney interrupted his thoughts as he realized he was hurriedly cramming her suitcase into the trunk of the taxi even though they had plenty of time to get to the airport before their flight.

"Christmas party at the bookshop."

"I suppose I'm your guest then."

"I suppose you are."

"Oh, Sammy-Finns, you couldn't be sweeter if you tried."

*Sidney Montgomery, age fifteen, clutching a ten-year-old
Sam Finney to her as he patted her pregnant belly*

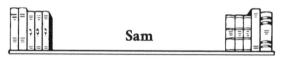

Sam

About a week before the Christmas book club party, AJ came to
Sam. "Hey, Sam, I need some help."

"Yeah? Where's Matthew?"

"Gone."

Sam eyed her with a curious expression that she wasn't sure how
to read. Immediately, she tried to mask any feelings she might be wearing on her own face. She missed Matthew a lot, and not just when it
came to hanging up door signs.

"I just want you to hang something up for me above the door to
the shop," she went on.

"Sure." He locked the door to the deli and followed AJ to 32 Aspen
Court, where Ivy was at the ready with a wobbly wooden ladder and a
heavy wooden sign to match. Tall as Ivy was, she couldn't reach above
the double doors of the old Victorian mansion and wouldn't have been
able to lift the sign up even if she could. Still in his apron, with tomato
juice and avocados spread down his front, Sam climbed up the ladder
and reached down to the girls who, together, hefted it up to him.

He spent some time under the porch roof adjusting the length of the chain so it was above the door but a patron couldn't miss seeing it as they entered the store. When he was done, he climbed down and stood back to admire his handiwork. The sign was so large, you could still read it even if you were on the Green.

Rejoice and be Glad.

"Amen," Sam mumbled.

"Thanks." AJ slapped him on the back, getting him in the kidneys due to their height difference.

When Sam saw Sidney walk through the door in the middle of the Christmas gathering, arm-in-arm with Matthew, he was surprised to find he was happy to see her. AJ was ready now, he thought. She could stand on her own two feet again. Now was as good a time as any, too. Not even Sid could ruin a night like this. Everyone was on a contentment high.

Sid looked tense, standing there, nervous even. But when she met Sam's gaze across the room, she visibly relaxed. If Sam Finney was smiling at her—if that once young boy she'd disappointed could forgive her—surely she had a shot with AJ. Sam made his way to Sidney, looking all out of place in holey jeans and knee-high boots among the layers and layers of Victorian garb on everyone else.

Matthew, too, was so very Matthew in his typical lumberjack attire. AJ couldn't have missed them if she tried, but she hung back a minute and waited anyway when she spotted Sam walking over to them.

Sam tipped his top hat. "Welcome home." Sidney nearly melted with relief. "Now close that door, you're letting the snow in."

"AJ." Sidney found her daughter. "Matthew invited me. I hope . . ."

"It's fine, Mom. It's fine." She hugged her mother for the first time in a long time. The brooch AJ was wearing with her costume stabbed her in the neck a little, so she let go a little sooner than Sidney wanted. There was an awkward moment of untangling arms while her mother still hung on.

"Go put your bags in your room and stay awhile." AJ pursed her lips and finally said something she should have said years ago. "Please."

Matthew started to follow Sidney out of the door to grab both their luggage.

"Matthew." She caught his hand with her left, and his thumb touched where the gold band used to be. "Thank you for dragging her back."

He held her hand tight for a minute, both of them relishing the physical contact. He then leaned in and kissed her cheek before disappearing out the door to get the bags. AJ's cheek tingled, and she smiled.

It was enough. It was more than enough for now.

> "Every one of us strive to be better, to be bold. Keep striving.
> That is how we honor the legacy that is Kevin Rhys."
>
> *Pastor Carson at Kevin Rhys' funeral*

Nancy

Lady Harrigan, of course, was as happy as a clam. First of all, people were treating her like royalty, and who couldn't love that? She felt like a queen in her long silk skirts, all fuchsia with pink rosettes over white lace on the trim. She'd even found vintage leather high-heeled boots in pink with the old-fashioned laces. Who would have thought?

"This is nice, Nancy," Ann said. "This is real nice." A compliment from Ann just sent Nancy over the moon. Ivy was waltzing around, looking like a gothic bar wench, but the girl had a real zest for life, and though she and the girl bickered like crazy, she was really starting to love the little gypsy who'd settled down and made a home in Lily Hollow.

Ah, and there came Matthew and Sidney through the door, a perfect ending to their perfect week. Seeing Matthew and AJ would be adorable. Seeing Maude reunite with her daughter would be interesting, too. Maude was off loitering in the westerns, avoiding actual human contact. But she was wearing a costume! Nancy had triumphed.

As much as the old hag grumbled about Jack, she'd loved her father, and she missed him terribly these days. They'd been steadfast companions for so long, raising her daughter and then her granddaughter together. Nancy thought it must be lonely living in that old house now, so she'd introduced Maude to the no-longer-widows-only club.

Then there was Matthew and AJ. Nancy eyed AJ as she watched Matthew enter the service elevator. She suspected what those two would be up to later, then shamed herself for the thought. Matthew disappeared behind the grated door with Sidney, and Nancy saw AJ turn her attention to Maude.

The music was festive, the tree was gorgeous, the scones were out-of-this-world delicious, Harper Jay had been caught spiking the cider, and Nancy was in love with her boots. She tapped her toes in a little happy dance under her skirts. She loved these skirts.

"The moon rose high while the sun was still out – streaked the sky purple and orange. Coyotes howled, and the horses obediently walked the trails, nodding their heads with the rhythm of their pace. It didn't matter what had been before as long as the cowboy could go out looking at a sunset like this."

from Cowboy Moon, *by Jack Walters, published in 1978*

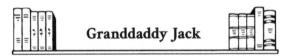

Granddaddy Jack

Anna Jane, my darling girl,

If you're reading this, I have passed. No tears. I've had a great life. I loved my Emma with all my heart, I did my best as a father, and I've been blessed by my grandchildren.

I've left you the hotel and all my book royalties. Don't worry about everyone else, they'll have their share. Your old great granddad did a good job, kiddo. I'm a proud and happy man. There's a journal, our notebook, our dreams for the hotel. In your own time, the building is there. Just remember it was your dream first, so don't give up on it, not even for Kevin.

One more thing: take care of Abigail Lacey. She's been kind to our family through the years. It will be her time soon; someone should be there for her.

This town needs a spruce, my dear. Nothing spruces like 32 Aspen Court when she's happy. There's magic in her bones.

J. Walters

"It's a good old building, Abby. She'll keep."

Jack Walters to Abigail Lacey
the day Maude closed the hotel doors.

Acknowledgments

Many thanks to my wonderful husband Jonathan, our beautiful daughter, and my Lord and Savior Jesus Christ . . . You guys are who make life worth living.

Thanks to Jennifer Joy Golightly and my own Emily Strange (Murillo), you two have kept me sane and writing, each in your own ways. To my best friend, Danielle, who reads and listens to everything I throw at the world. To my sister and mom, who both taught me how to read and write in the first place.

Thanks to Lolly Davis, the first person I remember telling me I should write. Too bad I don't have a copy of *Younger Squirrel's Fur.*

Thanks to Jacob Cartwright for helping me navigate html when this story was merely a writing exercise on a blog.

Thank you, Katie Lavois, my personal editor and future co-author.

Thanks to everyone who believed in this story.

About the Author

A.K. Klemm lives in Texas with her husband, daughter, and hounds. *The Bookshop Hotel* series is an ode to her years spent at Half Price Books in Humble and one of her favorite stores called Good Books in the Woods.

She is a wife, a mother, a dog lover, a retired bookseller and buyer from a used bookstore, a third degree black belt and martial arts instructor, forager, aspiring cyclist, a Christian, a sister, an aunt, a college graduate, a movie making enthusiast, oh yeah... and a bibliomaniac.

Connect with A. K.

Email:	andiklemm@rocketmail.com
Facebook:	facebook.com/AnakalianWhims
Web:	anakalianwhims.wordpress.com
Twitter:	@ AnakalianWhims

Grey Gecko Press

Thank you for reading this book from Grey Gecko Press, an independent publishing company bringing you great books by your favorite new indie authors.

Be one of the first to hear about new releases from Grey Gecko: visit our website and sign up for our New Release or All-Access email lists. Don't worry: we hate spam, too. You'll only be notified when there's a new release, we'll never share your email with anyone for any reason, and you can unsubscribe at any time.

At our website you can purchase all our titles, including special and autographed editions, preorder upcoming books, and find out about two great ways to get free books, the Slushpile Reader Program and the Advance Reader Program.

And don't forget: all our print editions come with the ebook free!

www.GreyGeckoPress.com

Support Indie Authors & Small Press

If you liked this book, please take a few moments to leave a review on your favorite website, even if it's only a line or two. Reviews make all the difference to indie authors and are one of the best ways you can help support our work.

Reviews on Amazon, GoodReads, GreyGeckoPress.com, Barnes and Noble, or even on your own blog or website all help to spread the word to more readers about our books, and nothing's better than word-of-mouth!

http://smarturl.it/review-bookshop

Recommended Reading

Chickens & Hens
by Nancy-Gail Burns

When young Marnie unexpectedly loses her father, her grandmother moves into her home to help her mother and all three women must create a new life together—all while Marnie goes through the trials of adolescence in 1960s small-town America.

Marnie witnesses unexpected lessons—from the heartwarming to the hilarious—learned by family and townsfolk. She also sees the older women in her life fall in love again. But will Marnie ever find true love herself... or has she missed the most important lesson of all?

Find out in this delightful story of three women who will make you laugh, make you cry, and above all, make you proud to be a woman.

Seashells, Gator Bones, and the Church of Everlasting Liability
Stories from a Small Florida Town in the 1930s

by Susan Adger

In the 1930s, the fictional town of Toad Springs, Florida, is filled with the adventures and daily whatnots of worthy, down-to-earth folk such as Flavey Stroudamore, owner of a three-legged gator named Precious who also just happens to have a birthmark of Jesus on his side.

Joining Flavey are Buck Blander, pastor of the Church of Everlasting Liability, who honed his preaching skills in prison but doesn't tell his parishioners, and Sweetie Mooney, whose attempt to run a beauty shop in her aunt's home fails after tragedies with head lice and henna hair dye.

This lively, heartwarming collection of tales from the Sunshine State will inspire you to smile!